D0111214

Library of Congress Cataloging in Publication Number: 2010925367

ISBN: 978-1-59474-453-2

Printed in China
Typeset in Berthold Akzidenz Grotesk

Designed by Jenny Kraemer
Production management by John J. McGurk

Distributed in North America by Chronicle Books
680 Second Street
San Francisco, CA 94107

10 9 8 7 6 5 4 3 2 1

Quirk Books
215 Church Street
Philadelphia, PA 19106
www.irreference.com
www.quirkbooks.com

DisneySTROLOGY

What Your Birthday Character Says About You

BY LISA FINANDER

INTRODUCTION

Welcome to the exciting world of *Disneystrology*! Drawing on the wisdom of astrology, numerology, and tarot, this book matches characters from your favorite Disney and Disney/Pixar movies with a certain day of the year. When you look up your birthday, you'll find the character that shares personality traits and distinctive abilities with you. You'll discover what makes that character so unique and, in turn, what makes *you* unique. In addition, each birthday character will offer you guidance for that day—the day your story began. Not only will you learn about your strengths and capabilities, you'll also be given tips for unlocking your ultimate potential.

It doesn't matter if you are female and your character is male, or vice versa. Magic is magic; it knows no gender. You can use these talents to embark on your very own heroine's or hero's journey.

Disneystrology is much more than a birthday book—it's filled with 366 days of fun and enchantment. In addition to looking up your birthday and those of your friends and family, you can use this fun compilation to find out which character will preside over special occasions, such as baby showers, anniversaries, and graduations. You can also use *Disneystrology* as a book of days to become aware of what gifts each day holds, allowing that information to guide you throughout your daily activities. Plus, Disney and Disney/Pixar birthday characters provide great inspiration for creating theme parties, choosing children's bedroom decor, or anything else you can dream up.

Are you ready to enter a world of joy, possibility, and, of course, magic? Well then, come on, let's go on an adventure! Don't forget to bring along your sense of wonder and curiosity.

Once upon a time, on a very spectacular day unlike any other, you were born and . . .

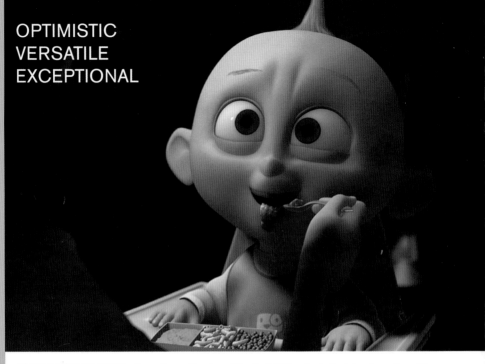

OPTIMISTIC
VERSATILE
EXCEPTIONAL

JACK-JACK PARR You have the enthusiasm and determination to reach your goals. It doesn't take long for others to notice your super-human achievements, because what comes naturally to you sets you apart from your peers. Uninhibited and inventive, you like trying different approaches just to see what happens. Sometimes just being you can confound less imaginative people, but that doesn't stop you from enjoying life or having fun.

Magical Gifts: Jack-Jack bestows the gift of unlimited potential. With his guidance, you can progress from ordinary to extraordinary in no time.

Keys to Your Success: Having the freedom to develop your innate abilities.

Jack-Jack's Story: *The Incredibles* (2004)

EEYORE You are reserved and highly observant. You crave attention but don't actively seek it. When others go out of their way to let you know how special you are to them, you experience true joy, and your outlook toward the world becomes cheerier. Underneath that gray exterior is a loving, loyal person with a warm heart, eagerly waiting for an opportunity to shine.

Magical Gifts: Eeyore gives you the gifts of compassion, humbleness, and commitment. He encourages you to use your awareness to notice all the wonderful things in the world.

Keys to Your Success: Having loving friends to celebrate life with.

Eeyore's Story: *Winnie the Pooh and the Honey Tree* (1966)

JANUARY 3

PROTECTIVE
FIERCE
ADORING

MRS. JUMBO You are creative and nurturing. What you yearn for eventually happens. You cherish children, nature, and imagination. Brave and gentle, you hold on tight when someone or something touches your heart. You stand up for what you believe in, always ready to make sacrifices and fight hard for those you love. You are filled with pride for loved ones, and your devotion inspires them to do amazing things.

Magical Gifts: Mrs. Jumbo teaches you about the endless power of love. She gives you the gifts of humor, tenderness, and courage.

Keys to Your Success: Tempering your passion so that others can understand and support your actions.

Mrs. Jumbo's Story: *Dumbo* (1941)

CARL You plan for the future. You are a collector, surrounding yourself with objects that remind you of your goals and keep your vision alive. It takes you a while to warm up to new people and ideas but once you do, you are totally committed to them. In fact, your partnerships with others are what motivate you to achieve your cherished desires.

Magical Gifts: Carl gives you the gifts of loyalty, endurance, and creativity. He encourages you to keep your heart open to the spirit of adventure.

Keys to Your Success: Enjoying the journey as much as the destination.

Carl's Story: *Up* (2009)

GRATEFUL
SENSITIVE
HARD-WORKING

SNEEZY You respond physically to the conditions of your environment. But that doesn't keep you from accomplishing your objectives, and you always bounce back. You are surrounded by good friends who try to lessen the effects of hindrances you face. Inquisitive and sensible, you always do your best to support others and fulfill your responsibilities.

Magical Gifts: Sneezy gives you the gifts of optimism, kindness, and stamina. He teaches you to become aware of what makes you feel bad and what makes you feel good.

Keys to Your Success: Enjoying the camaraderie of good friends.

Sneezy's Story: *Snow White and the Seven Dwarfs* (1937)

KENAI You are strong in mind, body, spirit, and heart. The bonds you form with loved ones are so deep that they influence your actions. Because you follow your instincts when making important decisions, you must ask yourself which emotion is driving you. Even though you try to do things alone, companionship is where you discover your deeper truth. In your life, you will experience many mystical occurrences.

Magical Gifts: Kenai bestows the gifts of love, spirituality, and courage. He teaches you the importance of understanding different points of view before taking action.

Keys to Your Success: Valuing your human and animal natures.

Kenai's Story: *Brother Bear* (2003)

JANUARY 7

HUMBLE
SENSITIVE
PERSISTENT

MADELLAINE You practice hard until you master the skills needed for success. You are receptive to the opinions of others, which influence your beliefs about yourself. Therefore, it is important to surround yourself with positive and nurturing people. Gentle persuasion helps you blossom and increase your self-confidence. In relationships, the love you share with others is transformative.

Magical Gifts: Madellaine bestows the gifts of tenderness, acceptance, and adaptability. Ask her for help whenever you want to turn difficulties into strengths.

Keys to Your Success: Seeing the real beauty in yourself and in others.

Madellaine's Story: *The Hunchback of Notre Dame II* (2002)

SCAT CAT You fill your days doing the things you love. Surrounding yourself with like-minded individuals who share your passion and intensity for creative expression, you attract many admirers. You are loyal, and your friends know they can always count on your help. The strength of your character is often enough to keep opponents at bay. When it isn't, you turn up the heat.

Magical Gifts: Scat Cat brings the gifts of leadership, fun, and a special dose of coolness. Call on him whenever you need help getting out of a tricky situation.

Keys to Your Success: Protecting and supporting others.

Scat Cat's Story: *The Aristocats* (1970)

JANUARY 9

CAPABLE
PERCEPTIVE
HONEST

MITTENS You have a resilient spirit and are able to maneuver both the joys and the challenges of life. With every setback you develop new abilities, and with every victory you surround yourself with more love. You are practical, witty, and helpful. Tough on the outside, you are patiently waiting for the right person to cross your path to share your affection.

Magical Gifts: Mittens teaches you that love never really leaves, it just shows up in different forms. She bestows the gifts of sensitivity, courage, and wisdom.

Keys to Your Success: Knowing that an open heart is more powerful than a closed one.

Mittens's Story: *Bolt* (2008)

BAGHEERA You learn from experience and solve problems logically. But that doesn't mean you're aloof. On the contrary, you are concerned about the wellbeing of others, and that is exactly why you make tough decisions. Love and admiration are important to you, but you rarely ever profess your love openly, except in certain circumstances. You are clever and witty.

Magical Gifts: Bagheera bestows the gifts of responsibility, thoughtfulness, and discernment. He guides you to see the truth in every situation and to communicate it honestly.

Keys to Your Success: Letting people see your tender side more often.

Bagheera's Story: *The Jungle Book* (1967)

PROUD
CAPABLE
RATIONAL

LI SHANG You have a lot going for you. You are strong, intelligent, disciplined, and calm. These qualities perfectly suit you for positions of leadership. You follow the rules to achieve your goals. When something challenges your beliefs, you can be stubborn. Fortunately, your compassion for those you care about softens your convictions. Underneath your reserved persona lies a gentle heart.

Magical Gifts: Li Shang bestows the gifts of dedication, serenity, and thoughtfulness. Ask Li Shang to guide you in balancing the needs of your mind and heart.

Keys to Your Success: Knowing that your best strategies result from having an open mind and heart.

Li Shang's Story: *Mulan* (1998)

SAMSON You have integrity, and people admire you. You are competitive but caring. Because it is important to you to maintain the respect of others, you don't always share how you truly feel. You are fearless in your devotion to your family, and trusted friends support you in your search for authenticity. A natural storyteller, you enjoy recounting heroic tales to inspire and impress others.

Magical Gifts: Samson bestows the gifts of compassion, encouragement, and creativity. He reminds you to be proud of who you are and where you came from.

Keys to Your Success: Letting others get to know the real you.

Samson's Story: *The Wild* (2006)

**FEISTY
COURAGEOUS
LOYAL**

SERGEANT TIBS You are clever and capable in a crisis. You work well with others, but it is often your ideas and actions that make the greatest difference in people's lives. Always aware of your environment, you allow your keen instincts to show the quickest path to success. You are compassionate and make great sacrifices, even for those you don't know well.

Magical Gifts: Sergeant Tibs brings the gifts of intelligence, perception, and heroism. With his assistance, you can free yourself and others from precarious situations.

Keys to Your Success: Aiding those who are unable to help themselves.

Sergeant Tibs's Story: *101 Dalmatians* **(1961)**

REBELLIOUS
SEARCHING
AESTHETIC

JANUARY 14

MELODY You are determined and driven. Once you set your mind on something, nothing but practical experience can change it. Although intellect helps you achieve your goals, it can also get you in trouble. Your family is important even though you feel restricted by them at times, and you look for places where you are free to be yourself. You cherish animals and enjoy their companionship.

Magical Gifts: Melody bestows the gifts of determination, inquisitiveness, and courage. She shows you how to fulfill your heart's many longings.

Keys to Your Success: Discovering where you feel most at home.

Melody's Story: *The Little Mermaid II: Return to the Sea* (2000)

IMAGINATIVE
DYNAMIC
COMPELLING

SIR GILES You are idolized because of your courage and willingness to help those in need. You are an excellent storyteller, and your mythic tales inspire others. Not one to back down from adventure, you want to experience life first-hand. Sometimes your larger-than-life reputation keeps others from getting to know the real you. Fortunately, all you require to be happy is a few close friends who share your interests.

Magical Gifts: Sir Giles bestows the gifts of wisdom, experience, and creativity. Under his guidance, your contributions to society are sure to be legendary.

Keys to Your Success: Showing the world that our similarities are more important than our differences.

Sir Giles' Story: *The Reluctant Dragon* (1941)

DOC HUDSON You possess considerable talent and have a strong desire to serve others. You appear confident, but inside are memories of defeat that haunt you. Once able to appreciate your past and the fact that life has sent you in a different direction, you can use your life lessons to mentor others. Mysterious, proud, and alluring, you put on quite a show.

Magical Gifts: Doc bestows you with the gifts of achievement, spirituality, and ingenuity. A creative and compassionate soul, Doc encourages you to open yourself more to others.

Keys to Your Success: Letting go of past disappointments.

Doc's Story: *Cars* (2006)

JANUARY 17

WISE
STRAIGHTFORWARD
RESPONSIBLE

AKELA You have foresight and make compassionate decisions. Rather than hiding from the truth, you listen to opposing viewpoints before embarking on a course of action. Others rely on your leadership, and you fulfill obligations with poise and diplomacy. Always striving to be your best, you possess great discipline. You're sensitive to the needs of others and happiest when you resolve problems with a win-win solution.

Magical Gifts: Akela bestows the gifts of good judgment, thoughtfulness, and guidance. Seek his counsel when choosing a path that benefits everyone.

Keys to Your Success: Ensuring the safety of your pack.

Akela's Story: *The Jungle Book* (1967)

THUNDERBOLT You have certain innate talents that give you an advantage over your peers. Others look up to you, and your image inspires them to pursue their potential. Having friends who stand by you in good times and bad helps you become the hero you only imagined yourself to be. Your presence brings joy and hope to the lives of others.

Magical Gifts: Thunderbolt bestows the gifts of creativity, courage, and friendship. Whenever you forget what you're capable of, he will remind you of all the amazing things you've already accomplished.

Keys to Your Success: Going on a real adventure.

Thunderbolt's Story: *101 Dalmatians II: Patch's London Adventure* (2003)

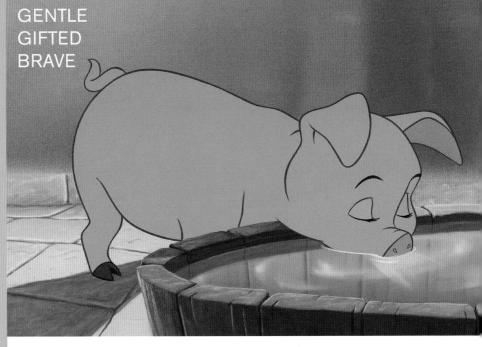

GENTLE
GIFTED
BRAVE

HEN WEN You may appear ordinary but you possess remarkable talent. Caring, tender, and wise, you don't flaunt your abilities. Because you're sensitive to environmental forces, it's important for you to be with those who respect and understand your trusting nature. You prefer the simple things in life and enjoy letting others pamper you.

Magical Gifts: Hen Wen gives you the gift of vision. With her help, she will lovingly guide you in the direction of your dreams.

Keys to Your Success: Revealing your mystical talents to the right people.

Hen Wen's Story: *The Black Cauldron* (1985)

ENDURING
ECCENTRIC
IMPULSIVE

LIZZIE You are witty, relationship oriented, and nostalgic. You aren't afraid to say what's on your mind even if it shakes things up. Because your perspective differs from the outlooks of those around you, it sometimes appears as if you're in your own world. You're good natured and like to have fun and make people laugh. No matter your age, you're bold and want to be part of the action.

Magical Gifts: Lizzie bestows you with the gifts of longevity, community, and curiosity. With her help, your classic look will always be in style.

Keys to Your Success: Finding your bliss and sticking with it.

Lizzie's Story: *Cars* (2006)

CHARISMATIC
RESOURCEFUL
BRIGHT

JAKE You are the best at what you do and enjoy performing these skills for others. You're daring, think quickly on your feet, and improvise when necessary. Others are often awestruck by your abilities, and when with you they know they're in capable hands. On the outside you're upbeat and carefree, but underneath you're keenly aware of your environment.

Magical Gifts: Jake bestows the gifts of bravery, self-assurance, and allure. He will provide you with the knowledge and practical skills needed to master your surroundings.

Keys to Your Success: Using your appetite for adventure to benefit others.

Jake's Story: *The Rescuers Down Under* (1990)

GOPHER You like to engineer dynamic devices to make your work easier. Your mind moves quickly from one idea to the next, delving beneath the surface to understand how things work. Although you intend to help others, some of your techniques can be precarious. Combining originality with time-tested techniques brings you success.

Magical Gifts: Gopher offers the gifts of imagination, speed, and spontaneity. With Gopher's guidance, you can manifest many useful endeavors all at once.

Keys to Your Success: Using the right amount of power for the job.

Gopher's Story: *Winnie the Pooh and the Honey Tree* (1966)

WISE
UNCONVENTIONAL
HUMOROUS

MAMA ODIE You are one of a kind, knowledgeable in the workings of the universe and of the human psyche. Although you tend to be a private person, you graciously help those in need. Longevity and devotion to your craft make your services desirable and respected. You are happy being yourself and encourage others to be as well.

Magical Gifts: Mama Odie bestows the gifts of perception, empathy, and light-heartedness. Through her guidance, you will see the truth in all situations.

Keys to Your Success: Using your powers to help others fulfill their destinies.

Mama Odie's Story: *The Princess and the Frog* (2009)

BUZZ LIGHTYEAR People marvel at your capabilities. Because your talents come effortlessly, you set high standards and become frustrated when you're unable to live up to the image that others have of you. Once you become aware of your limitations and realize that no one is perfect, your life is enriched. Your friends prove that the real you is superior to any gadget or device you possess.

Magical Gifts: Buzz brings the gifts from the intergalactic alliance: originality, bravery, and vitality. If you have a problem that requires an out-of-this world solution, call on him.

Keys to Your Success: Discovering your authentic self.

Buzz's Story: *Toy Story* (1995)

JANUARY 25

PREVAILING
LOYAL
CONSIDERATE

SARABI You are outspoken. When others are in trouble, you voice your opposition. You aren't afraid to fight against evil, but at the same time you are sweet, caring, and attentive to loved ones. A supportive and capable partner, even in times of personal hardship you have a warm and open heart. Patient and wise, you know that in time the truth will be revealed.

Magical Gifts: Sarabi bestows the gifts of tenderness, devotion, and bravery. Ask her for guidance when you are apprehensive about speaking your truth.

Keys to Your Success: Being true to yourself.

Sarabi's Story: *The Lion King* (1994)

STITCH You are a one-of-a-kind power-house of intensity. You have more energy than you can contain, and you feel compelled to express it. It is your chosen method of expression that can get you into trouble. When you choose to, you have an amazing ability to transform situations and people for the better. Your deepest desire is to belong, and once you find someone who loves you, you will risk everything to preserve that relationship.

Magical Gifts: Stitch bestows the gifts of vigor, intelligence, and individuality. He shows you how to master the art of gentleness and intimacy.

Keys to Your Success: Learning to control your mischievous urges.

Stitch's Story: *Lilo & Stitch* (2002)

NOVEL
FRIENDLY
EXUBERANT

CLANK AND BOBBLE You bring joy to everything you do. Being part of a group in which your talents are needed and appreciated provides you with the support and encouragement you require to develop your expertise. You have an active mind and keep yourself energized by implementing your many ideas. A loyal and easygoing friend, people can always count on you to cover for them in a pinch.

Magical Gifts: Clank and Bobble give you the gifts of graciousness, optimism, and potential. Playful and loving, they will help you discover the vocation that suits you best.

Keys to Your Success: Putting your natural abilities to good use.

Clank and Bobble's Story: *Tinker Bell* (2008)

FLIK You dream big. Your mind is not limited by convention and the way things have always been. You can see the need for change in restrictive or archaic situations, even though you don't always know how to make it happen. With patience and help from a few trusted allies, you enrich and empower the lives of an entire community.

Magical Gifts: Flik's gifts are innovation, compassion, and determination. He encourages you to trust your judgment and stick to your plans.

Keys to Your Success: Believing in yourself when no one else does.

Flik's Story: *A Bug's Life* (1998)

ATTENTIVE
EAGER
FEISTY

FIGARO You are mischievous and like to work alongside your friends. You are not a pushover, by any means, but you will inconvenience yourself at times to assist others. In return, you receive love and attention. Playful and affectionate, you enjoy experiencing life on your own terms. When no one else is looking, you have been known to sneak a treat.

Magical Gifts: Figaro bestows the gifts of curiosity, self-confidence, and warmth. He will teach you how to maintain your independence while living with others.

Keys to Your Success: Making friends with all kinds of people and creatures.

Figaro's Story: *Pinocchio* (1940)

THE DOORKNOB You are clever and witty. Chaotic environments do not adversely affect you; rather, they allow you to remain welcoming and focused on the present. You have an unusual way of assisting those who feel distressed. Instead of providing straight-forward solutions to their problems, you help them think their way out of their predicament. You are persuasive, possess good judgment, and enjoy intellectual humor.

Magical Gifts: The Doorknob gives you the gifts of optimism, independence, and curiosity. Ask for his assistance whenever you need some levity and perspective in your life.

Keys to Your Success: Taking turns expressing your opinions.

Doorknob's Story: *Alice in Wonderland* (1951)

ARTISTIC
CARING
HARD-WORKING

HORATIO FELONIOUS IGNACIOUS CRUSTACEOUS SEBASTIAN You have exceptional talents and display them in prominent venues. Because your work is vitally important, you take your duties very seriously. You form loving friendships with those you mentor. Young people bring out your softer side and influence your beliefs. Witty, sentimental, and intelligent, you are happiest when people get to know the person behind the genius.

Magical Gifts: Sebastian gives you an appreciation and expert ability for artistic expression, especially through music. Call on him when you want to professionally develop your creativity.

Keys to Your Success: Supporting others through their significant life transitions.

Sebastian's Story: *The Little Mermaid* (1989)

MERRYWEATHER You are a quick thinker and like to take charge of situations. You have strong opinions, and once a method works you see no reason to try something new. In your mind, the more efficient you are in getting your work done, the more time you have to play. Spirited and imaginative, you put your own personal mark on everything you do.

Magical Gifts: Merryweather sprinkles you with the magic gifts of insight, intelligence, and swift action. If you need her guidance, try wearing something blue to get her attention.

Keys to Your Success: Diminishing the unkind actions of others.

Merryweather's Story: *Sleeping Beauty* (1959)

CURIOUS
OPTIMISTIC
RESPONSIBLE

THE CAPTAIN You are a steward of the earth. Dedicated to serving those entrusted to your care, everyone benefits from your executive abilities. Usually, you're laid-back and refrain from questioning the intentions of your advisors. But when you see an error being made, you spring into action and can accomplish heroic feats. You are resourceful and love teaching others the skills required to become self-sufficient.

Magical Gifts: The Captain brings the gifts of awakening, leadership, and purpose. With his guidance, you can return to your true home.

Keys to Your Success: Recognizing that artificial intelligence is not the same as wisdom.

The Captain's Story: *WALL•E* (2008)

LARS You have your own aesthetic impression of the world, which you want to share with others. Certain subjects capture your attention, and you explore them from every angle. You are strong in your beliefs; if something or someone you care about is threatened, you courageously defend them. Intelligent and gentle, you form lasting relationships only with those who share your visions.

Magical Gifts: Lars brings the gifts of insight, compassion, and steadfastness. Call on him when you need the discipline and daring to pursue your dreams.

Keys to Your Success: Standing up for what you believe in.

Lars's Story: *101 Dalmatians II: Patch's London Adventure* (2003)

ATYPICAL
SMART
OUTSPOKEN

LILO Society's norms frustrate you at times. You have the same needs as everyone else: love, acceptance, and recognition. But people expect you to be like they are and follow the rules. Of course, you can't; your sense of the world is completely different. As you grow, you learn to channel your energies into activities that constructively and effectively bring your insights and wisdom into the world.

Magical Gifts: Lilo bestows many gifts: originality, feistiness, sincerity, will power, and 'Ohana. She encourages you to embrace the idiosyncrasies in yourself and in others.

Keys to Your Success: Becoming aware of your impact on others.

Lilo's Story: *Lilo & Stitch* (2002)

MADAME ADELAIDE BONFAMILLE

Many choices and opportunities are available to you. You are very loyal, valuing friendship and companionship above all else. You have a good memory and are sentimental. Because you enjoy culture, the arts, and life's finer things, you seek like-minded persons to experience them with. Optimistic and generous, you are warm-hearted and more than willing to devote your time and means to causes you believe in.

Magical Gifts: Madame Bonfamille bestows the gifts of prosperity, intuition, and empathy. In all your endeavors, she will bring you grace and gentleness.

Keys to Your Success: Using your resources wisely.

Madame Bonfamille's Story:
The Aristocats (1970)

TALENTED
ADMIRED
MOTIVATING

WOODY You take the lead and are proud of your place in the world. Optimistic and sensible, you aid others through encouragement and reassurance. Since you have a big heart, you're able to overcome any feelings of insecurity and befriend others. Once you discover that even those you idolize have self-doubts, you become instrumental in boosting the self-confidence of those around you.

Magical Gifts: Woody brings you the gifts of imagination, distinction, and adaptability. Whenever you feel unsure about yourself, Woody is there to remind you that you are worthy and loveable.

Keys to Your Success: Knowing that you are irreplaceable.

Woody's Story: *Toy Story* (1995)

REBELLIOUS
UNCONVENTIONAL
IDEALIST

FILLMORE You strive to bring your vision of the world into existence. You believe in equality, freedom, and green living. Because you are sentimental about the past and dream of a perfect future, the present can be the most difficult place for you to be. Your friends and your livelihood keep you grounded. It takes a while for people to warm up to your ideas.

Magical Gifts: Like Fillmore, you are interested in making the world a better place for everyone. He bestows the gifts of independent thinking, humor, and inclusiveness.

Keys to Your Success: Living your life in a way that supports and reflects your beliefs.

Fillmore's Story: *Cars* (2006)

FEBRUARY 8

SENSITIVE
INTUITIVE
RESERVED

SALLY You are imaginative. You are good with your hands and use your creativity to make practical items. Your heart yearns for fulfillment, and you become restless when you feel trapped. Insightful, you sense the motivations and needs of others. You form friendships with unique individuals whose desires and thoughts are similar to your own. When in love, you gain the confidence to move toward your aspirations.

Magical Gifts: Sally bestows the gifts of premonition, empathy, and ingenuity. Ask her for guidance when you are contemplating future goals.

Keys to Your Success: Believing that things will turn out okay.

Sally's Story: *Tim Burton's The Nightmare Before Christmas* (1993)

THE PUPPIES You are full of energy and want to be part of the action. Brave and resilient, you can lead as well as follow. You like adventure but also the comforts of home. Because you are adaptable, you make the best of any circumstance and always come out ahead. People find you endearing and offer assistance in your time of need. Family members can rely on your love and loyalty.

Magical Gifts: The Puppies bestow the gifts of contentment, enjoyment, and sociability. In their eyes, we are all one big happy family.

Keys to Your Success: Sticking together as a group.

The Puppies' Story: *101 Dalmatians* (1961)

FEARLESS
VIVACIOUS
AFFECTIONATE

BOO You are undaunted and cheerful. Instinctively, you choose the right people to help you achieve your desires. You are curious and enjoy exploring new places. Sometimes you're unaware of the underlying circumstances surrounding your situation. Nonetheless, your playful and warm nature has a powerful effect on the emotions of others and makes them want to protect and care for you at all costs.

Magical Gifts: Boo bestows the gifts of adventure, adaptability, and friendship. She encourages you to trust yourself because you're braver than you think.

Keys to Your Success: Laughing at your fears.

Boo's Story: *Monsters, Inc.* (2001)

REMY There is no one quite like you. You are a talented freethinker. The limits of humanity cannot keep you from pursuing your dreams. Because you're a visionary, when you reach your goal, everyone benefits. Even though it takes a while for people to accept you and your ideas, be patient. Soon you'll receive the support and recognition you desire.

Magical Gifts: Remy gives you the gifts of genius, initiative, and well-developed senses. He encourages you to study what you love most.

Keys to Your Success: Pursuing your passion, no matter how outrageous it appears to others.

Remy's Story: *Ratatouille* (2007)

FEBRUARY 12

LOVING
BRAVE
TENACIOUS

KIARA You positively change the lives of those in your environment. If something doesn't make sense, you tend not to believe it and rely on your own intuitive knowledge. You're strong-willed and like to have fun. Instead of focusing on the differences among people, you focus on the similarities. Through your love and acceptance of others, you change the world one person at a time.

Magical Gifts: Kiara bestows the gifts of honor, wisdom, and compassion. Call on her protection when you need guidance in fulfilling your destiny.

Keys to Your Success: Restoring order in the places where disagreement reigns.

Kiara's Story: *The Lion King II: Simba's Pride* (1998)

RANJAN You have an active imagination and seek adventure. You idealize the heroic acts of others and want to emulate them. Confident, determined, and optimistic, you are fearless and resourceful in the face of danger. As a result, you emerge victorious in almost everything you attempt. You are playful, have a big heart, and are interested in the people and world around you.

Magical Gifts: Ranjan bestows the gifts of joyfulness, creativity, and courage. Under his supervision, you can safely explore new and exciting places.

Keys to Your Success: Accompanying and defending those you care for.

Ranjan's Story: *The Jungle Book 2* (2003)

FEBRUARY 14

MISCHIEVOUS
ENERGETIC
BOLD

GURGI You express yourself openly and easily. You like to have fun and entertain others. Eager to please, you don't always realize the enormity of the responsibilities you agree to take on. At times, you focus solely on attending to your physical needs. But at crucial moments your emotions take over, and your actions reflect the profound devotion you have for loved ones.

Magical Gifts: Gurgi bestows the gifts of inquisitiveness, companionship, and self-lessness. Whenever you feel afraid, Gurgi reminds you that your love for others will make you brave.

Keys to Your Success: Forming friendships that last a lifetime.

Gurgi's Story: *The Black Cauldron* (1985)

MAURICE You are interested in unusual things. You enjoy sharing your creations with others. Easily distracted by new ideas, you can get into trouble when you aren't paying attention to what's going on around you. Close relationships are important to you because they provide the love and support you need to do your life's work.

Magical Gifts: Maurice bestows the gifts of ingenuity, faithfulness, and adventure. He encourages you to let your mind explore far-off places while keeping the rest of you close to home.

Keys to Your Success: Taking good care of both you and your loved ones.

Maurice's Story: *Beauty and the Beast* (1991)

CURIOUS
GOOD-HEARTED
AMICABLE

TAD, PEARL, AND SHELDON You notice the qualities that make each of us unique. Because you are genuinely accepting of these differences, your friends are able to be themselves around you and know there is a place where they belong. Everything in life interests you, and you are excited to be part of the action. You learn through experience, and you aren't afraid to try new things or take calculated risks.

Magical Gifts: Tad, Pearl, and Sheldon bring the gifts of observation, spontaneity, and inclusiveness. Call on them for encouragement whenever you're ready for new adventures.

Keys to Your Success: Turning obstacles into opportunities.

Tad, Pearl, and Sheldon's Story: *Finding Nemo* (2003)

UNWAVERING
VISIONARY
SPIRITED

PABLO You are sensitive to the needs of your body. If unable to enjoy your environment, you focus all your energies on finding a new one. Although others support your endeavors, it is your own resourcefulness and creativity that allow you to attain your goals. You are patient and daring, perfecting your ideas through trial and error.

Magical Gifts: Pablo brings the gifts of exploration, ingenuity, and success. He reminds you that each failure brings you one step closer to realizing your aspirations.

Keys to Your Success: Moving to the place where you feel most comfortable.

Pablo's Story: *The Cold-Blooded Penguin* (1945)

GENTLE
PHILOSOPHICAL
PATIENT

RUFUS You understand the mechanics of faith. You know that favorable outcomes happen in time and that all of us are worthy of happiness. As a service-oriented individual, you nurture those who feel uncertain and alone. You notice the beauty in others and make a point to share it with them. People trust your judgment and value your friendship.

Magical Gifts: Rufus gives the gifts of serenity, wisdom, and compassion. When you need his guidance, offer a few cat treats and he will come and lift your spirits.

Keys to Your Success: Reassuring others when they have lost hope.

Rufus's Story: *The Rescuers* (1977)

FISH OUT OF WATER You express yourself through actions. You don't just imagine traveling to exotic locations; you do it. Fearless, you gather and create the essentials needed to explore unfamiliar places. Working on your inventions in solitude, you emerge only after you've perfected the device. You love life and want to experience as much of it as possible.

Magical Gifts: Fish Out of Water brings the gifts of aptitude, cooperation, and resourcefulness. Travel with him to meet new friends and visit exciting places.

Keys to Your Success: Communicating with others in your own way.

Fish Out of Water's Story: *Chicken Little* (2005)

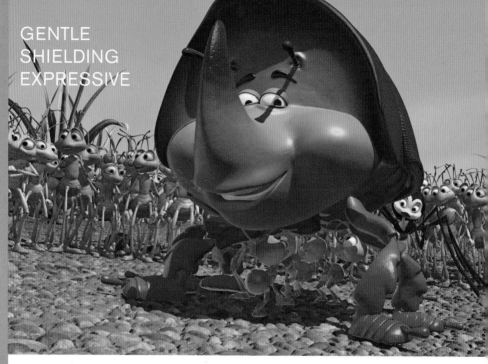

GENTLE
SHIELDING
EXPRESSIVE

DIM You are caring and giving, which makes you irresistible to children. You help those in trouble, often sacrificing your own safety. Sometimes you wish you could hide your feelings, but that's not who you are. Intuitively gifted, you know what others need and provide it to them.

Magical Gifts: Dim's gift is the ability to feel and act upon emotions in the moment. With him as your guide, you are sure to have a brave and loving friend.

Keys to Your Success: Realizing the importance of your efforts to the welfare of the group.

Dim's Story: *A Bug's Life* (1998)

SENTIMENTAL
PROTECTIVE
SHY

RED You experience the world through your heart. You take great care and put considerable energy into maintaining and sustaining your creations. Friendship and closeness are vital to your well-being. You're observant and take your time getting to know someone before revealing all your feelings. Having a tranquil home restores your vitality.

Magical Gifts: Red bestows the gifts of emotional depth, tenderness, and generosity. Call on him when planting the seeds for a beautiful garden—literally or figuratively—that you want to thrive.

Keys to Your Success: Belonging to a group in which you play an integral part.

Red's Story: *Cars* (2006)

FEBRUARY 22

WISE
POWERFUL
COMPASSIONATE

MUFASA You put the needs of the community above your own. An enlightened teacher, you have much to share and offer. Those around you benefit greatly from your affectionate and protective nature. Because you seek to bring out the best in everyone, you're surprised when someone betrays you. Idealistic, you have high aspirations for yourself and your loved ones.

Magical Gifts: Mufasa bestows the gifts of family, leadership, and valor. He teaches you to respect life and to remember that we are all connected.

Keys to Your Success: Understanding that people change only if they truly want to.

Mufasa's Story: *The Lion King* (1994)

ELASTIGIRL (aka Helen Parr) You live your life to the fullest. You are successful both at work and at home. Sometimes you spread yourself too thin trying to do everything perfectly. You're nurturing, confident, and prepared. Throughout life, you'll have the chance to play many roles, and you approach each one with maturity and wisdom. In partnerships, you won't settle for anything less than equality.

Magical Gifts: Elastigirl bestows the powers of optimism, loyalty, and strength. Her guidance allows you to meet any challenge, with or without superpowers.

Keys to Your Success: Making sure that others stretch to meet your needs, too.

Elastigirl's Story: *The Incredibles* (2004)

FEBRUARY 24

PERSEVERING
ARTISTIC
IDEALISTIC

PRINCE CHARMING You are self-reliant, modest, and refined. Determined but not aggressive, you stay on course. People often project their fantasies onto you, but you remain astute and quickly dismiss those with selfish motives. You are patient and unafraid to search for what is most important to your heart. Creative pastimes appeal to your romantic nature.

Magical Gifts: Prince Charming provides, well, charm. He bestows the gifts of diplomacy, altruism, and perception and encourages you to find what you need to live happily ever after.

Keys to Your Success: Choosing people who love you for who you really are.

Prince Charming's Story: *Cinderella* (1950)

CODY You devote yourself to defending those who cannot defend themselves. You have a special connection to and respect for nature. Because you're gentle and loving with animals, you've earned their trust. You can sometimes overestimate your ability to do things alone and may fall into traps set by others. You attract like-minded friends who support your cause. Curious and brave, you fill your days with adventure.

Magical Gifts: Cody gives you a profound respect for all of life. He will teach you how to communicate and act as a steward for the natural world.

Keys to Your Success: Soaring with the eagles.

Cody's Story: *The Rescuers Down Under* (1990)

MAGICAL
UPLIFTING
DEDICATED

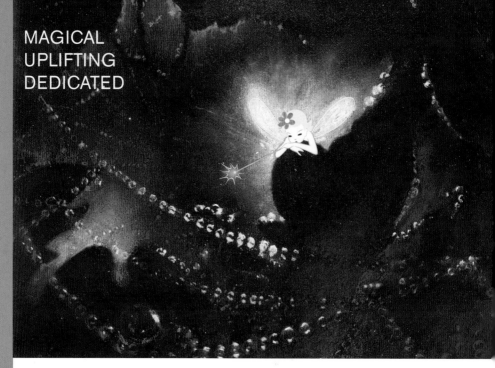

THE DEWDROP FAIRIES You live your life from a higher perspective. Whatever you touch fills with beauty and wonder. Highly imaginative, your mind concentrates on ways to bring more joy and vitality into the world. Your talents are extraordinary, and you perform them effortlessly. Whenever you're working on a task, you listen to music that helps you concentrate. You're benevolent and service-oriented, and your efforts support and benefit everyone.

Magical Gifts: The Dewdrop Fairies bestow the gifts of mystery, radiance, and creativity. When you want your achievements to sparkle, they will gracefully assist you.

Keys to Your Success: Enlivening others with your light.

Dewdrop Fairies' Story: *Fantasia* (1940)

SMART
GIVING
ELEGANT

NEERA You are protective of those you love. You're equally loyal to both your friends and family, and that can cause problems if not everyone is on the same side. A strong and capable partner, you will fight alongside your friends for the greater good of your community. Your calm demeanor and playful sense of humor charm others.

Magical Gifts: Neera gives you the gifts of understanding, tenderness, and rationality. Ask for her guidance when you're questioning alliances.

Keys to Your Success: Realizing that, even when you care for people, they may make choices you can't mend.

Neera's Story: *Dinosaur* (2000)

ENTHUSIASTIC
CONFIDENT
DRAMATIC

RHINO You have a wild imagination that can get you into trouble. You believe in heroes and heroines, that good always wins, and that anything is possible (even if others think it's impossible). In other words, your inner child is alive and thriving. You're a clever person; even when your dreams turn out to be illusions, you achieve them anyway. When you put all your tremendous energy into creative expression, it's guaranteed to be magical.

Magical Gifts: Rhino shows you that life is exciting. He gives you the gifts of willpower, optimism, and spontaneity.

Keys to Your Success: Knowing that wishful thinking does not always change the facts.

Rhino's Story: *Bolt* (2008)

CHESHIRE CAT You are insightful and helpful in an idiosyncratic way. Because your birthday appears and disappears depending on the year, you have your own relationship with time and aging. Youthful in appearance and demeanor, you are mischievous and your pranks produce random results. Although you may look unusual to others, you perceive that they, not you, are the ones behaving strangely.

Magical Gifts: Cheshire Cat bestows the gifts of uniqueness, mystery, and intelligence. He suggests celebrating your birthday only when you want to become a year older and having fun the rest of the time.

Keys to Your Success: Leaving with a smile.

Cheshire Cat's Story: *Alice in Wonderland* (1951)

COMPETENT ARTISTIC SENSITIVE

ANITA RADCLIFFE You are a visual person who takes great care in your appearance. Your public image is respectable and refined, but that's only part of who you are. With loved ones, you show your emotional side, which is deep and caring. Playful, sensible, and thoughtful, you enrich the lives of those you care for.

Magical Gifts: Anita bestows the gifts of creativity, devotion, and a love for animals. Her greatest blessing is that someday a puppy or other animal will become your friend.

Keys to Your Success: Filling your home with music, laughter, and the company of caring and trustworthy companions.

Anita's Story: *101 Dalmatians* (1961)

DANNY You are talented at the art of make-believe. You take ordinary experiences and reimagine them into wonderful sagas. Your creativity lifts everyone's spirits, including your own. Sensitive to your surroundings, you grow upset when loved ones are unhappy. Personal relationships are important, and you look up to those you care about. You encourage others to believe in themselves and their dreams.

Magical Gifts: Danny gives you the gifts of happiness, hope, and enthusiasm. He teaches the importance of never being too grown-up or busy to enjoy life.

Keys to Your Success: Keeping the magical tales of your childhood alive.

Danny's Story: *Peter Pan In Return to Never Land* (2002)

HAPPY
EMPATHETIC
FREE-SPIRITED

SILVERMIST You have a compassionate and offbeat view of society. You're in tune with your environment and dislike loud noises and disharmony in your personal space. Believing that everyone should get along, you do your best to create peaceful dynamics at work and at home. You use your intuition and imagination to bring beauty and positive energy into the world.

Magical Gifts: Silvermist bestows the gifts of friendship, individuality, and sympathy. Call on her whenever you need a gentle push to follow the yearnings murmuring deep inside.

Keys to Your Success: Helping fish (or friends) swim upstream.

Silvermist's Story: *Tinker Bell* (2008)

WART (young King Arthur) You put your heart and soul into everything you do. You are unassuming and worry about performing your job perfectly. Sometimes you put the wishes of others above your own. It's important for you to have people in your life who guide you toward fulfilling your potential. You trust the wisdom of others, and they believe in you.

Magical Gifts: Wart brings you the gifts of wonder, sacrifice, and thoughtfulness. He teaches you to have faith in yourself and courageously follow your path, wherever it leads.

Keys to Your Success: Claiming your rightful place in the world.

Wart's Story: *The Sword in the Stone* (1963)

INTENSE
REGIMENTED
COMMUNICATIVE

THE MARCH HARE You have an ironic sense of humor and natural comedic timing. You adore wordplay and brainteasers and choose friends who share your passion. But you're not as light-hearted as you appear, and often your silliness results from feeling frazzled. Incisive, you do your best to avert trouble. You have an active mind and imagination, and these creative energies need an outlet to keep you from going crazy.

Magical Gifts: The March Hare bestows the gifts of inquisitiveness, expressiveness, and duality. He encourages you to celebrate life every day.

Keys to Your Success: Staying positive in your own zany way.

The March Hare's Story: *Alice in Wonderland* (1951)

SNOW WHITE You have an ethereal quality that charms and draws others to you. Although you come from a powerful lineage, you choose a simpler life that follows the path of your soul. You are visual, and you create a home that is lovely, clean, and uncluttered. When faced with difficult people or circumstances, you accept what is and promise yourself that everything will be all right. You are gentle, cheerful, and undaunted by hard work.

Magical Gifts: Snow White gives you a rich dream life, magnetism, and sense of humor. She teaches the power inherent in receptivity.

Keys to Your Success: Your befriending and adoring nature.

Snow White's Story: *Snow White and the Seven Dwarfs* (1937)

OPTIMISTIC
INNOCENT
SPELLBOUND

THE LOST BOYS You have a childlike quality and a strong connection to your youth. Playful, with a penchant for daydreaming, you imagine yourself embarking on wondrous adventures. You look for mentors and successful people to emulate. Finding friends who exert a constructive influence in your life allows you to put your artistic and intuitive talents to practical use.

Magical Gifts: The Lost Boys courageously bring you a treasure chest of gifts: friendship, loyalty, kindness, joy, ingenuity, and cheerfulness. They remind you that you're never alone.

Keys to Your Success: Going on voyages that enliven your youthful spirit.

The Lost Boys' Story: *Peter Pan* (1953)

GISELLE You experience life from more than one reality. Depending on the company you keep, you can feel totally lost and out of place or right at home. You develop self-awareness by spending time in distant places with people whose beliefs are radically different from your own. Because you're able to merge fantasies with practical knowledge, you succeed in obtaining the best of both worlds.

Magical Gifts: Giselle bestows the gifts of originality, imagination, and daring. She helps you gather your cherished dreams and bring them into your every-day existence.

Keys to Your Success: Expressing all your emotions in order to become more real.

Giselle's Story: *Enchanted* (2007)

LAID-BACK
INQUISITIVE
ENDURING

CRUSH AND SQUIRT You trust life and are interested in experiencing new things. Every adventure increases your wisdom and reinforces your beliefs. Making friends comes naturally, and you have a reassuring effect on others. Through your actions and achievements, people learn more about themselves and their world. You're optimistic and perceptive, and you like to have fun. Family members especially benefit from your unconditional love and support.

Magical Gifts: Crush and Squirt bestow the gifts of exploration, unselfishness, and confidence. They can't wait to escort you toward your coolest dreams.

Keys to Your Success: Helping others reach their destination.

Crush and Squirt's Story: *Finding Nemo* (2003)

KODA Your need to love and be loved is strong. You like the intimacy of conversation because you're eager to understand people's similarities and differences. Both humans and animals are attracted to your spirited and affectionate nature. You profoundly affect those who care for you by bringing out their nobler qualities.

Magical Gifts: Koda bestows the gifts of storytelling, wisdom, and trust. Call on him when you need a companion to help you discover the true meaning of your totem.

Keys to Your Success: Letting others figure certain things out for themselves.

Koda's Story: *Brother Bear* (2003)

FAITHFUL
EXCEPTIONAL
NURTURING

NANA You have a talent for discerning what others need. Intelligent and intuitive, you know better than anyone what's really going on in the lives of loved ones. You're protective, efficient, and kind. Family members adore you and cherish your company. There is more to you than meets the eye, and only special people see the entirety of who you are and what you can do.

Magical Gifts: Nana bestows the gifts of wisdom, tenderness, and reliability. No matter what your breed, she will watch over you and help you grow.

Keys to Your Success: Enriching the lives of those you love.

Nana's Story: *Peter Pan* (1953)

WYNKEN, BLYNKEN & NOD You are wise beyond your years. Smart and worldly, you use your aptitude to experience different levels of consciousness. You work well with peers and make sure everyone is safe and accounted for before moving forward. Your future is as bright and vast as your imagination.

Magical Gifts: Wynken, Blynken & Nod bestow the gifts of faith, wonder, and magic. They encourage you to explore novel ideas and to follow your dreams wherever they lead.

Keys to Your Success: Knowing the value of having your head in the clouds.

Wynken, Blynken & Nod's Story: *Wynken, Blynken & Nod* (1938)

LIVELY
JOYFUL
INQUISITIVE

CHIP You are fascinated by a world that's full of unexpected surprises. Early on, you became aware of how one person's self-centeredness can affect the fate of so many. Yet you remained cheerful and feisty through it all. Instead of letting hard times get you down, you allow them to spark your curiosity. You investigate every detail of each new situation, and your presence makes life more fun.

Magical Gifts: Chip bestows the gifts of wonder, tenacity, and courage. He teaches you not to back away from any of the opportunities that life presents.

Keys to Your Success: Working with others to effect positive change.

Chip's Story: *Beauty and the Beast* (1991)

RESTLESS
HONEST
IDEALISTIC

MARCH 14

RYAN You strive to emulate your personal heroes and heroines. You imagine the characteristics and knowledge you must possess to live up to their image. As a result, you can be hard on yourself, forgetting that mastering a skill takes time. Through experience, you become aware of your capabilities and view others and yourself more realistically and compassionately. You're aware of your emotions and express them freely.

Magical Gifts: Ryan brings the gifts of integrity, clarity, and spiritedness. He will help you move out of another's shadow and into your own light.

Keys to Your Success: Following your own path to greatness.

Ryan's Story: *The Wild* (2006)

IDEALISTIC
CAPTIVATING
ASSURED

PRINCE EDWARD You believe in your ability to succeed. You're unafraid to show your talents to the world, and you charm and entertain others with your lofty outlook. People may question your rationality, but they soon realize you can accomplish feats they never imagined. You're in love with life and throw yourself completely into your endeavors.

Magical Gifts: Prince Edward bestows the gifts of faith, resiliency, and dramatic flair. No matter how outlandish your ideas might seem to others, he will escort you to your dreams.

Keys to Your Success: Going to the places where true love lives.

Prince Edward's Story: *Enchanted* (2007)

MIRACULOUS
FAIR
BENEVOLENT

THE BLUE FAIRY You possess inner as well as outer beauty. Receptive to the needs of others, you hear their pleas and remedy their situation in an unconventional manner. You never let people become dependent on you; instead, you guide them in achieving their desires through wise decision making. You watch over those you care about and only intervene when absolutely necessary.

Magical Gifts: The Blue Fairy gives you profound insight into the workings of the world. Through her, you will understand the mystery of magic and inspire others to reach their highest potential.

Keys to Your Success: Exposing lies wherever they grow.

The Blue Fairy's Story: *Pinocchio* (1940)

**BRAVE
ENTHUSIASTIC
DETERMINED**

BLAZE You form strong attachments with those you love. You're happiest when you can be of service and demonstrate your heroism and capabilities to others. There are only a few things you're afraid of, and you avoid encountering them as much as possible. People who adore you love spending time in your company. You enjoy being part of exciting adventures and can't wait for the next one to begin.

Magical Gifts: Blaze brings you the gifts of compassion, cheerfulness, and cooperation. Invite him into your life, and he will bring light to everything you do.

Keys to Your Success: Showcasing your talents to the world.

Blaze's Story: *Tinker Bell* (2008)

FLOWER You are empathetic, intuitive, and endowed with a rich dream life. You need quiet, uninterrupted time to rejuvenate and take care of yourself while avoiding unpleasant and overcrowded places. Introspective and gentle, you live life at your own pace. You form lasting friendships, are a good listener, and always return to the places and people you love.

Magical Gifts: Flower teaches the importance of rest and following the natural cycles of the seasons by enjoying extroverted activities in the warmer months and introverted pursuits in the winter.

Keys to Your Success: Letting the path of the sun be your guide.

Flower's Story: *Bambi* (1942)

CURIOUS
FRIENDLY
DETERMINED

NEMO You can't wait to be on your own. You think others worry about you need-lessly. Headstrong and bright, you're eager to meet new people and learn new things. Loved ones like having you around; that's one of the reasons they're so protective of you. Your cheerful and extroverted personality quickly grants you access into new groups.

Magical Gifts: Like Nemo, you long to see the world and meet new people. Nemo's gifts are courage, cooperation, trust, and a "lucky fin."

Keys to Your Success: Considering the wisdom of others along with your own.

Nemo's Story: *Finding Nemo* (2003)

PRINCESS AURORA You enjoy being out in nature. You possess artistic talents, which you use to enhance the beauty of your surroundings. Nonaggressive, you make your displeasure known through emotion and seclusion. People misinterpret your soft-spoken approach as vulnerability, and yet, blessed with good fortune, you emerge victorious. You strive to balance duty with your need to choose for yourself.

Magical Gifts: Princess Aurora bestows the gift of awakening to your dreams as a mature adult. Let her guide you to bring out the majesty you imagine into the world.

Keys to Your Success: Singing the song in your heart.

Princess Aurora's Story: *Sleeping Beauty* (1959)

MARCH 21

FAITHFUL
AFFECTIONATE
GENUINE

PLUTO You try to balance your desires with the needs of others. You form strong bonds with those you love and are protective of them. Playful and friendly, you communicate your feelings honestly and spontaneously. You know the difference between right and wrong and can be hard on yourself when you let others down. People and animals adore your loving and tolerant nature.

Magical Gifts: Pluto bestows the gifts of conscience, kindheartedness, and mischief. He is a loyal friend who will provide you with unconditional love.

Keys to Your Success: Following the advice of the good angel sitting on your shoulder.

Pluto's Story: *The Moose Hunt* (1931)

DASH You have a competitive spirit. You want to see how your capabilities compare to those of others and discover how far they can take you. Your boundless energy is no match for those around you and can get you into trouble if you don't have a constructive outlet for it. Life is an exciting adventure, and you enjoy being part of a unique family.

Magical Gifts: Dash bestows the gifts of cleverness, success, and enthusiasm. If you need to accomplish something amazing, he'll be there before you even ask.

Keys to Your Success: Realizing that there are speeds other than fast, faster, and fastest.

Dash's Story: *The Incredibles* (2004)

MARCH 23

INTELLIGENT
CONCERNED
WILLFUL

OLIVIA FLAVERSHAM You are a quick thinker and use these abilities to care for others. You make friends easily and win their allegiance through your persistence and charm. In difficult times, you are prone to fretting. But because you want to be part of the solution, you overcome your fears and accomplish whatever you set out to do. Curious and capable, you're cherished by loved ones.

Magical Gifts: Olivia bestows the gifts of shrewdness, courage, and kindness. When you're worried and need to think clearly, call on her to come up with a brilliant strategy.

Keys to Your Success: Finding the right allies to help you.

Olivia's Story: *The Great Mouse Detective* (1986)

DOPEY You are lighthearted and genial. You express yourself physically and can be quite silly. Because you're thoughtful and interested in love more than money, people often underestimate your cleverness and ability to get what you want. You let your heart inspire you to create anything that brings you joy, whether music, dance, or inventing new games. You're youthful and adaptable, and your smile lights up the room.

Magical Gifts: Dopey brings the gifts of friendship, fun, and spiritedness. With him as your guide, you'll never lose your sense of wonder.

Keys to Your Success: Entertaining others by simply being you.

Dopey's Story: *Snow White and the Seven Dwarfs* (1937)

FUN
CONFIDENT
ENTHUSIASTIC

TIGGER You never run out of energy. You're optimistic, creative, and charming. Because you're so sure of yourself and your abilities, you're shocked when things don't turn out as planned. You usually discover, after the fact, that the things you can't do, you don't like to do anyway. You never lose your childlike innocence and are shy around those you admire. Your best friends are the ones who appreciate your energy and spontaneity.

Magical Gifts: Tigger bestows everything that Tiggers like: a happy heart, good friends, and a fabulous bouncing ability.

Keys to Your Success: Looking before you bounce.

Tigger's Story: *Winnie the Pooh and the Blustery Day* (1968)

NURTURING
INTELLIGENT
AMUSING

HUGO, VICTOR, AND LAVERNE

You have many sides to your personality. Depending on the circumstances and the people involved, you can be dignified, mischievous, or persuasive. Spending time alone and away from the action allows you to gain perspective. You're accepting of others, and they depend on your friendship and kindness. A private individual, you reveal yourself only to trusted companions whose company you respect and enjoy.

Magical Gifts: Hugo, Victor, and Laverne bestow the gifts of wisdom, enthusiasm, and protection. When in need of compassionate advice, call on them for guidance.

Keys to Your Success: Having fun with your closest friends.

Hugo, Victor, and Laverne's Story: *The Hunchback of Notre Dame* (1996)

TALENTED
ENCOURAGING
PRACTICAL

PHILOCTETES You are interested in achieving excellence in everything you do. Knowledgeable and worldly, you're a demanding but exceptional teacher. Dreams of success keep you motivated even if previous attempts provided disappointing results. You hide your emotions under a tough shell, but you are a loyal, enthusiastic, and concerned friend.

Magical Gifts: Phil brings the gifts of vitality, skill, and persistence. When you need a mentor to help you reach your goals, Phil is there to drive you forward.

Keys to Your Success: Working with the gods until you reach your goals.

Phil's Story: *Hercules* (1997)

KRONK You are trusting and eager to help others. You prefer direct and honest interaction over innuendos or covert communication. In all situations, you're diligent and serve others with your own unique style. Because you perceive the world through your senses, your genius lies in the artistic realm, where you can give form to your imaginings. Children and animals benefit from your gentle and attentive nature.

Magical Gifts: Kronk bestows the gifts of creativity, tenderness, and physical ability. He encourages you to cultivate your creative talents and share them with others.

Keys to Your Success: Dedicating your energy to nourishing pursuits.

Kronk's Story: *The Emperor's New Groove* (2000)

FEISTY
TRUTHFUL
ENTHUSIASTIC

GRANDMOTHER FA You are not afraid to be yourself. You're decisive and follow your hunches. In most situations, you speak your mind and state the obvious with humor. You're perceptive and can easily read the intentions of others. When it comes to your loved ones, you'll do anything to help them achieve happiness. Mischievous, independent, and eccentric, you inspire others to be themselves.

Magical Gifts: Grandmother Fa bestows the gifts of intuition, loyalty, and genuineness. Whenever you need help accomplishing the impossible, call on her to provide unconventional assistance.

Keys to Your Success: Sharing the secrets of good fortune.

Grandmother Fa's Story: *Mulan* (1998)

IMAGINATIVE
UNWAVERING
EAGER

CHICKEN LITTLE You allow your perceptions to operate outside everyday awareness. At first, it's difficult for you to act on your discoveries; but your determination helps you succeed. You work diligently to fulfill your goals, and your closest allies are the ones who support your efforts, even when still untested. Although many of your ideas are ahead of your time, people eventually come to understand your visions and value your accomplishments.

Magical Gifts: Chicken Little bestows the gifts of open-mindedness, resiliency, and compassion. He reminds you that many geniuses were considered crazy in the beginning.

Keys to Your Success: Never giving up on what you know is true.

Chicken Little's Story: *Chicken Little* (2005)

CLEVER
DETERMINED
OPTIMISTIC

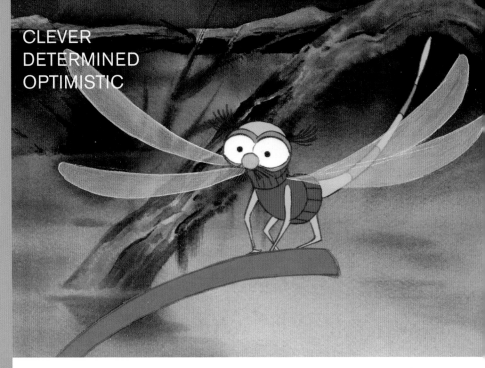

EVINRUDE You have incredible stamina and always finish what you start. People admire your exceptional athletic abilities, and you use these talents to help others. Feisty, you can outsmart any adversary or obstacle. When you're most in need of encouragement, friends come through and cheer you on to victory. You're expressive, and others easily understand what you're feeling.

Magical Gifts: Evinrude gives the gifts of strength, awareness, and leadership. Whenever you need to get somewhere fast, call on him; he's sure to give you an extra boost.

Keys to Your Success: Steering others in the right direction.

Evinrude's Story: *The Rescuers* (1977)

NANI You are a hard worker. You sacrifice your own needs for the benefit of others. Prone to worry and frustration, you try to manage the people and circumstances in your environment to keep life stable. Luckily, your earnest and tender nature enlists support from others. Your life is always interesting, and you enjoy it most when you take time to be carefree. You are resilient and sensitive to the needs of loved ones.

Magical Gifts: Nani bestows the gifts of devotion, wit, and adaptability. Ask for her assistance when taking on important responsibilities.

Keys to Your Success: Asking for help when you need it.

Nani's Story: *Lilo & Stitch* (2002)

SPONTANEOUS
LIGHTHEARTED
OBSERVANT

DALE You are imaginative, enthusiastic, and agreeable. Because you are easily distracted, you work best as part of a team. In fact, much of your time is devoted to partnering with others to meet your basic needs. You're clever and notice the little things often overlooked by those around you. When it comes to your friends, you are loyal and always up for adventure.

Magical Gifts: Dale gives you the gifts of curiosity, humor, and energy. Call on him when seeking more amusement and relaxation in your life.

Keys to Your Success: Working together to get the job done.

Dale's Story: *Test Pilot Donald* (1951)

PUMBAA You enjoy life's simple pleasures. Your friends are important to you, and you are uninhibited around them. At times you can act naïve, but others would be foolish to underestimate your cleverness or bravery. Most of the time you're easygoing and tend not to worry. But if someone you care for needs you, you're there in a heartbeat.

Magical Gifts: Pumbaa gives the gifts of genuineness, wit, and kindness. When you're feeling sad, ask him to help lift your spirits.

Keys to Your Success: Knowing when to take action and when to have fun.

Pumbaa's Story: *The Lion King* (1994)

ATTRACTIVE
NATURAL
ASSERTIVE

FALINE You are playful, intelligent, and a little bit wild. You're resourceful and unafraid to make the first move. Your inner and outer beauty draws others to you, which of course you use to your advantage. A romantic at heart, you nevertheless insist on maintaining your independence in relationships. Inquisitive and intense, you are interested in the people who inhabit your environment.

Magical Gifts: Faline gives you a love for the outdoors, athletic ability, and sparkle. Tell her what you want, and she'll help you go after it in a straight line.

Keys to Your Success: Taking turns going first.

Faline's Story: *Bambi* (1942)

NANNY You are an invaluable member of any family or business. You're skilled in a variety of areas, and no job is too big for you to handle with ease. You're full of energy, feisty, and down-to-earth. Those closest to you rely on your nurturing and expertise. Optimistic, you believe in love and that everything will turn out fine in the end.

Magical Gifts: Nanny gives the gifts of generosity, compassion, and courage. She is always ready to help you succeed; all you have to do is ask.

Keys to Your Success: Fighting for what you know is right.

Nanny's Story: *101 Dalmatians* (1961)

APRIL 6

INVENTIVE
CURIOUS
AFFECTIONATE

HUEY, DEWEY, AND LOUIE You love to explore the world around you. Because you're energetic, you require stimulating actives to keep you out of trouble. Endowed with cleverness, you especially like to play tricks on people to get their attention. It's important that your life includes special people who understand you and will always be there. Despite your occasional mischievous behavior, you are endearing to others.

Magical Gifts: Huey, Dewey, and Louie bring the gifts of vitality, camaraderie, and humor. They promise to look out for you on all your new adventures.

Keys to Your Success: Using your creative energy to assist others.

Huey, Dewey, and Louie's Story: *Hockey Champ* (1939)

SELF-ASSURED
IDEALISTIC
GENEROUS

LIGHTNING MCQUEEN You are in a hurry to get somewhere. Though your enthusiasm and innocence take you far, you'll inevitably come to realize that what you were seeking requires more than winning. You're a loving, optimistic person who appreciates creating a place to call home. Having friends who value you and willingly help you achieve a cherished goal is what makes you a champion.

Magical Gifts: Lightning brings the gifts of maturity, awareness, and authentic success. He encourages you to slow down and take an interest in the people around you.

Keys to Your Success: Discovering that no one succeeds alone.

Lightning's Story: *Cars* (2006)

LOVING
SENSIBLE
STRONG-MINDED

PENNY You are mature and dependable. You take your work seriously and often form meaningful friendships with coworkers. When work takes up too much time, you may begin to feel lonely. That's your clue to focus on what's most important. You follow your emotions and make wise decisions about your future happiness. Intuitive, you understand animals and enjoy their company.

Magical Gifts: Penny bestows the gifts of responsibility, conscience, and faithfulness. When you need a break, she suggests spending time with animals seeking your attention.

Keys to Your Success: Choosing to do what you love the most.

Penny's Story: *Bolt* (2008)

BUBBLES You surround yourself with the things you love. You're goal oriented and scrutinize your environment for opportunities to obtain more of what you desire. Group activities offer a sense of belonging and a chance to form friendships with those who'll look out for you. You're adept at finding beauty in the ordinary, and your expressiveness makes it easy for others to understand your feelings.

Magical Gifts: Bubbles brings the gifts of observation, joy, and determination. He is a great friend who will help you find and keep your buried treasure.

Keys to Your Success: Knowing what thrills you.

Bubbles's Story: *Finding Nemo* (2003)

APRIL 10

RESOURCEFUL
GRATEFUL
BRAVE

GUS & JAQ You are a quick learner and exceedingly versatile. You observe your surroundings and know when the time is right to make your move. Feisty and courageous, you take on momentous challenges that benefit the lives of those you love. Luckily, with the help of your friends, you conquer even the most perilous of situations. Whenever someone shows you kindness, you greatly appreciate the gesture and return the goodwill.

Magical Gifts: Gus & Jaq give you the gifts of shrewdness, creativity, and devotion. Request their compassionate and spirited assistance whenever you feel lonesome or defeated.

Keys to Your Success: Forming magical friendships.

Gus & Jaq's Story: *Cinderella* (1950)

WIDOW TWEED You are kind and powerful. Your strength lies in your ability to soothe people who are angry or fearful. Empathetic and willing to help, you foster others who have nowhere else to go. When it comes to those you love, you do what's best for them first. Those you care for feel safe and comforted by your presence.

Magical Gifts: Widow Tweed bestows the gifts of love, wisdom, and perception. She will give you the assertiveness to defend your values.

Keys to Your Success: Reconnecting with the memories of all the people, animals, and places that live in your heart.

Widow Tweed's Story: *The Fox and the Hound* (1981)

PROTECTIVE
ACTIVE
RESOURCEFUL

PIP It's crucial for you to be in environments where you can communicate effectively and be understood by others. Because you're astute and aware of people's intentions, you intervene if someone you care about needs help. You dislike deception and will reveal the truth regardless of consequences or personal risk. Your insights bring knowledge and awareness to people from many different lands.

Magical Gifts: Pip bestows the gifts of cleverness, spirit, and determination. He'll travel to distant places to help you live your dreams.

Keys to Your Success: Choosing the best world to live in.

Pip's Story: *Enchanted* (2007)

LEWIS You have a creative mind adept at coming up with solutions to complex and mundane problems. You're optimistic and have high hopes that your plans will work. When they don't, you grieve your losses and try again. Ultimately, you're working so hard because you want to make the world a happier place for everyone. You value family and friendship above all other achievements.

Magical Gifts: Lewis brings the gifts of ingenuity, insight, and kindness. He encourages you to use your imagination and never let failure hinder your success.

Keys to Your Success: Inventing a bright future.

Lewis's Story: *Meet the Robinsons* (2007)

DESTINED
CONSCIENTIOUS
THOUGHTFUL

PRINCESS ATTA Fate plays a strong role in your life. The subjects you study early on prepare you for your occupation as an adult. Responsible, cautious, and creative, you realize that your best friends are those who allow you to express your silly side. As you grow older, your life gets easier because you have learned to trust your own wisdom and abilities.

Magical Gifts: Atta brings you the gifts of awareness, courage, and open-mindedness. When presented with novel ideas, she teaches patience and encourages you to convince others to give it a try.

Keys to Your Success: Developing your own style of leadership.

Atta's Story: *A Bug's Life* (1998)

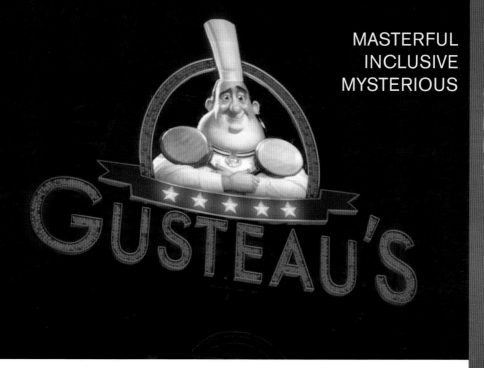

AUGUSTE GUSTEAU Your accomplishments influence the lives of many others. You endeavor to be the best and offer resources to people interested in learning your methods and gaining expertise. A true artist, you bring the muse of inspiration into your creations. Through your encouraging words and profound presence, you motivate others to achieve feats they never dreamed possible. Your imagination and generosity will take you far.

Magical Gifts: Auguste bestows the gifts of ingenuity, recognition, and mentoring. Under his guidance, you can learn time-honored techniques and infuse them with your own originality.

Keys to Your Success: Sharing your secrets with the world.

Auguste's Story: *Ratatouille* (2007)

JOYOUS
EXPRESSIVE
CURIOUS

HAPPY You bring warmth and optimism to your surroundings. You enjoy entertainment and like to amuse people. Only in the most serious of situations do you get the blues. But they don't last for long because you quickly dismiss your fears and focus on the positive. You're interested in the lives of others and bring enthusiasm to whatever you do, truly believing that laughter is the best medicine.

Magical Gifts: Happy brings you a heart that's open and filled with mirth. He encourages you to accept the foibles of your friends and have fun.

Keys to Your Success: Choosing joy as your companion.

Happy's Story: *Snow White and the Seven Dwarfs* (1937)

JOHN SMITH You have an avid interest in learning and exploring cultures different from your own. The mysteries of life appeal to you, and you want to understand the unknown. Brave and fervent, you are the first to embark on new experiences. Your personal relationships transform your ideas about the world. When you love someone, you will defend them publicly even if it makes you unpopular with your own group.

Magical Gifts: John brings the gifts of honesty, knowledge, and compassion. He encourages you to examine your own beliefs while remaining open to the views of others.

Keys to Your Success: Respecting the values and traditions of other people.

John's Story: *Pocahontas* (1995)

APRIL 18

POWERFUL
IDEALISTIC
DETERMINED

HERCULES You are on a quest to understand yourself. You have innate talents that separate you from your peers. Until you become comfortable with your powers and find a positive way to use them, you're unsure if they are an asset or a burden. Strong in both body and emotions, you do your best to help and please others. In the end, you choose the life that's best for you.

Magical Gifts: Hercules gives you the gifts of strength, compassion, and self-awareness. He will guide you to your rightful home in this world.

Keys to Your Success: Learning what it means to be a real hero or heroine.

Hercules's Story: *Hercules* (1997)

FAIRY MARY You are good at what you do and enjoy sharing your expertise with others. You're a good teacher but have little patience for those who don't take their work as seriously as you do. Because you appreciate your abilities and have a healthy dose of self-respect, you inspire others to do their best. Confident and proficient, you create a life that suits you perfectly.

Magical Gifts: Fairy Mary brings you the gifts of knowledge, self-control, and enthusiasm. When you're learning a new skill, she'll show you the simplest way to master it.

Keys to Your Success: Mentoring those who possess similar talents.

Fairy Mary's Story: *Tinker Bell* (2008)

WISE
RESPECTED
COMPASSIONATE

SITKA You have a profound understanding of life and its mystery. People admire this quality and seek your counsel. You use your leadership abilities to inspire, but not to dominate others. Love motivates your actions. No challenge is too big for you to overcome, and those you care for can always count on your support and diplomatic mediation. You are steady, self-aware, and fun loving.

Magical Gifts: Sitka bestows the gifts of guidance, spirituality, and devotion. He will show you your true path and help you become skilled at mentoring others.

Keys to Your Success: Guiding others toward their potential.

Sitka's Story: *Brother Bear* (2003)

DR. DAVID Q. DAWSON You are perceptive and a natural storyteller. You enjoy working with others and usually choose an associate with skills that complement your own. Cheerful, you make everyone around you feel better. Sometimes you get distracted and occasionally blunder, but it all works out in the end. You are the voice of reason that helps people accomplish their goals.

Magical Gifts: Dr. Dawson bestows the gifts of optimism, collaboration, and kindness. Whenever you feel blue, ask Dr. Dawson to cheer you up and escort you to your next destination.

Keys to Your Success: Changing your plans to assist another.

Dr. Dawson's Story: *The Great Mouse Detective* (1986)

APRIL 22

PERCEPTIVE
KIND
POWERFUL

THE EMPEROR Your words impact the lives of many. Revered for your wisdom, others count on you to remain calm as you guide them through difficult situations. You are self-aware, notice exceptional qualities in others, and act to modernize established beliefs. When the situation warrants, you will share your prized possessions to show your gratitude for the sacrifices others have made on your behalf.

Magical Gifts: The Emperor bestows the gifts of responsibility, clarity, and compassion. He will inspire you to lead others from a place of understanding, acceptance, and selflessness.

Keys to Your Success: Seeing the truth in every situation.

The Emperor's Story: *Mulan* (1998)

LADY People enjoy your company, and you completely devote yourself to those who love you and care for you. Your friends come from different backgrounds and you attempt to bring their worlds together. Loyal and committed, you don't change your mind easily, and you keep your promises. Partnerships that allow you to grow and experience new things are your best bet.

Magical Gifts: Lady gives you the gifts of enduring love, sophistication, and daring. She'll help you create a family that makes you feel secure and adored.

Keys to Your Success: Merging the need for freedom with a comfortable home.

Lady's Story: *Lady and the Tramp* (1955)

STRONG
TRUSTWORTHY
EXPERIENCED

MACK You like testing your limits. Knowledgeable and dedicated, you not only get the job done, but keep others organized as well. You value friendship, and you never give up on somebody in hard times. A true friend, sometimes you let others talk you into pushing yourself too hard on their behalf. You balance all that hard work by rewarding yourself with luxurious items.

Magical Gifts: Mack bestows the gifts of loyalty, responsibility, and abundance. He will help you stay committed to your profession and remind you to take time to enjoy yourself every now and then.

Keys to Your Success: Traveling in style.

Mack's Story: *Cars* (2006)

HEIMLICH You like comfort and are in touch with the needs of your physical body. At any age, you have a commanding presence and move through the awkward stages in life willingly and with a childlike innocence. You focus intensely on your future, knowing and believing that great things are in store for you. As a result, you center your day-to-day activities on preparing for that distant goal.

Magical Gifts: Heimlich bestows you with persistence, foresight, and friendliness. He encourages you to put your heart and soul into manifesting your dreams.

Keys to Your Success: Enjoying where you are at the moment.

Heimlich's Story: *A Bug's Life* (1998)

HUMOROUS
NATURAL
LEISURELY

RUTT AND TUKE You are earthy and enjoy nature and the outdoors. Your material tastes and habits are fixed; once you find a routine that works, you stick with it. In contrast, your mind is flexible and loves to engage in playful teasing. There's no rushing you, and you live life at a slow and pleasurable pace. You are devoted to loved ones and sensitive to their needs.

Magical Gifts: Rutt and Tuke bring the gifts of caring, wit, and ease. Call on them when you need to laugh and relax.

Keys to Your Success: Putting family first.

Rutt and Tuke's Story: *Brother Bear* (2003)

JENNY You are responsible and affectionate. You enjoy the company of a few close friends and protect those you love. The depth of your emotions is the source of your strength, and you will face your fears if someone you care about is in trouble. Playful and caring, you adore the companionship that your pets provide, and in return you give them a safe and loving home.

Magical Gifts: Jenny bestows the gifts of prosperity, compassion, and courage. Whenever you feel lonely, she will offer reassurance and perhaps bring along one of her furry friends to comfort you.

Keys to Your Success: Nurturing those in need.

Jenny's Story: *Oliver & Company* (1988)

INDOMITABLE
DEVOTED
WARM

LITTLE HOUSE You stay true to yourself amid change. The places where you feel the most contented are spacious, peaceful, and harmonious. Grandiose possessions don't impress you, and you're grateful for what you have. You are resilient and can overcome any setback. Both loved and appreciated by others, your style stands the test of time.

Magical Gifts: Little House gives the gifts of adaptability, independence, and joy. She reminds you that no matter what goes on in your world, you will attain happiness in the end.

Keys to Your Success: Holding your own ground.

Little House's Story: *The Little House* (1952)

COMMANDING
COMPASSIONATE
PARENTAL

THE GREAT PRINCE OF THE FOREST You have a powerful influence on your family. You are protective of those you care for and take your role in the family seriously. Even though it's hard for you to change when life requires you to take on new responsibilities, you do your best to adapt. Brave, loving, and forward-thinking, others look up to you and revere you as a source of inspiration and strength.

Magical Gifts: The Great Prince bestows the gifts of dignity, wisdom, and devotion. He will help you mature into your full potential.

Keys to Your Success: Letting loved ones experience your tenderness.

The Great Prince's Story: *Bambi* (1942)

MELLOW
ACCOMPLISHED
HAPPY

THE QUEEN You are a natural leader. Generous, easy-going, and funny, you have the ability to manage large projects and groups of people. Because you're patient, you know when the time is right to start a new venture. You're proud of your accomplishments and able to appreciate your successes. Loved ones admire and emulate you from a young age.

Magical Gifts: The Queen bestows the gifts of lightheartedness, intelligence, and prosperity. She encourages you to enjoy life and to satisfy your aspirations.

Keys to Your Success: Knowing when to let go and move on to the next stage.

The Queen's Story: *A Bug's Life* (1998)

MAID MARIAN You are able to see through appearances. You believe in justice, and you readily share your good fortune with others. Faithful and true, you form enduring relationships that begin in childhood. In romance, you choose partners with larger-than-life reputations. You, however, concentrate on their good intentions and support their endeavors. Difficult to fool, you understand the drives of loved ones.

Magical Gifts: Maid Marian bestows the gifts of friendship, awareness, and understanding. Ask for her guidance when you need help uncovering the truth in complex situations.

Keys to Your Success: Knowing which person is the one guilty of wrongdoing.

Marian's Story: *Robin Hood* (1973)

**DISCIPLINED
SENTIMENTAL
DEDICATED**

COLONEL HATHI You are most comfortable in positions of authority. You are responsible and try hard to bring out the best in everyone. You appear serious, but it's easy to see you have a tender heart and would do anything for those you love. Because you are headstrong, you seek partners who are equally tough and unafraid to voice their views.

Magical Gifts: Colonel Hathi gives the gifts of leadership, honor, and observation. Call on him when you need the power and perseverance to get the job done.

Keys to Your Success: Listening to the wisdom of family members.

Colonel Hathi's Story: *The Jungle Book* (1967)

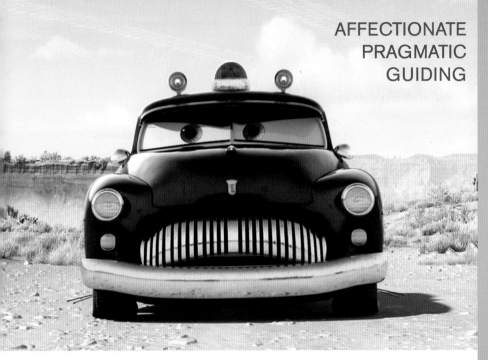

SHERIFF You are decisive and firmly believe in right and wrong. You have a classic style and perform your duties with ease. A natural-born mediator, you like to keep the peace. It takes you a long time to express your true feelings; but once you determine that a person is worthy of your trust, you will go the extra mile.

Magical Gifts: Sheriff bestows you with the gifts of confidence, sensitivity, and reliability. When you need to keep others in line, he'll help you lay down the law.

Keys to Your Success: Making time for rest and relaxation.

Sheriff's Story: *Cars* (2006)

LOVING
INQUISITIVE
TRUSTING

ALICE You are kind, well mannered, and outspoken. You hate to be bored, and your curiosity and eagerness to understand people and your surroundings have given you many remarkable experiences. Intelligent and observant, you notice when things aren't quite right. Sometimes you're a little gullible when it comes to other people's suggestions, but you're a quick learner and can maneuver your way out of disagreeable situations.

Magical Gifts: Alice bestows the gifts of cooperation, daring, and imagination. Ask for her assistance when those around you talk in riddles.

Keys to Your Success: Staying occupied without getting yourself into trouble.

Alice's Story: *Alice in Wonderland* (1951)

COBRA BUBBLES You apply traditional wisdom to unusual situations and see the steps required to rectify any problem. Surrounding yourself in an aura of mystery and power, you cannot be deceived. You communicate directly and swiftly get to the bottom of things. It takes time for others to realize that you keep an eye on them out of love and concern and not because you disapprove.

Magical Gifts: Cobra brings you the gifts of compassion, insight, and heroism. He will fearlessly look after you and those you love.

Keys to Your Success: Accepting the imperfections found in all families.

Cobra's Story: *Lilo & Stitch* (2002)

BENEVOLENT
COURAGEOUS
INTELLIGENT

BELLE You have an eye for authentic beauty. You enjoy learning and are imaginative. Even though you appreciate the comforts in life, they are not what drive you. Instead, you sacrifice your security for loved ones and choose companions who can match your level of devotion and loyalty. Feisty, you aren't afraid to ask for what you want and need. The strength of your love brings out the humanity in others.

Magical Gifts: Belle bestows the gifts of independence, determination, and individuality. Call on her when you need to break the spell of enchantment.

Keys to Your Success: Turning beasts into princes.

Belle's Story: *Beauty and the Beast* (1991)

DUMBO You form deep attachments with loved ones and work hard to ensure your family's security. Sincere, generous, and devoted, you never forget the kindness of others. There are times in your life when you may feel uncertain and doubt yourself, but your friends remind you of your remarkable abilities and give you hope. All it takes is for you to believe in yourself, and you'll soar to the top in no time.

Magical Gifts: Dumbo bestows the gifts of faith, resiliency, and guidance. When you feel stuck, Dumbo encourages you to look at the situation from a higher perspective.

Keys to Your Success: Knowing that you are exceptional.

Dumbo's Story: *Dumbo* (1941)

MAY 8

KNOWLEDGEABLE
CAPABLE
FAITHFUL

COGSWORTH You are good at managing large groups toward a common goal. You take your responsibilities seriously and do your best to keep everyone out of harm's way. Strong-minded, you require proof before altering an established method. When people take an interest in you, your temperament lightens, allowing you to show off your knowledge—in a dignified manner, of course.

Magical Gifts: Cogsworth brings the gifts of leadership, courage, and caring. Call on him for assistance when you're in a tough spot that requires guidance and patience.

Keys to Your Success: Making room in your life for the unexpected guest.

Cogsworth's Story: *Beauty and the Beast* (1991)

LITTLE JOHN You enjoy embarking on adventures with your friends that benefit society. You willingly defend and rescue those you care about. In the beginning, you perform your duties faithfully. Soon you realize that some of your causes might be a bit risky. When you question the intentions of your associates, you keep them honest.

Magical Gifts: Little John gives you the gifts of bravery, honesty, and humor. Whatever your goals, he is by your side to help you achieve them.

Keys to Your Success: Knowing if you're the good guy or the bad guy.

Little John's Story: *Robin Hood* (1973)

SMART
BRAVE
ENERGETIC

TOULOUSE You are determined to assert your independence. You love physical activities and possess athletic ability. Courage comes naturally to you, and you like to compete to see what you're capable of and how you measure up. Although you have artistic abilities, you resist developing them if you feel forced into doing so. You admire liberated and free-spirited people.

Magical Gifts: Toulouse offers the gifts of creativity, daring, and playfulness. He advises you to do things your own way and not worry about untidiness.

Keys to Your Success: Achieving your goals with the right amount of "fft, fft, fft."

Toulouse's Story: *The Aristocats* (1970)

JACK SKELLINGTON You have an unusual imagination. Because repetition bores you to death, you envision exciting adventures and are often oblivious to obstacles. Unless you find new sources of inspiration that allow you to create something new, you feel empty. You're excited to share your ideas with others, and those who care for you support your dreams even if they don't wholly understand them.

Magical Gifts: Jack bestows the gifts of curiosity, charisma, and tenderness. Ask for his guidance when you're feeling melancholy and need some otherworldly advice.

Keys to Your Success: Knowing which doors are yours to open.

Jack's Story: Tim Burton's *The Nightmare Before Christmas* (1993)

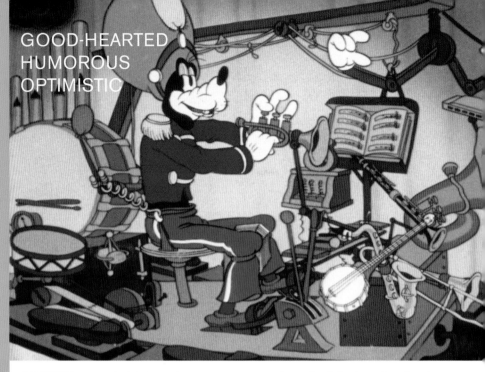

GOOD-HEARTED
HUMOROUS
OPTIMISTIC

GOOFY You are entertaining and care about others. You make people laugh and feel good. To you, life is a wondrous adventure, and you don't get upset if you make mistakes; you just smile and try again. People admire you for your willingness to attempt to learn new things. In everything you do, you are enthusiastic, humble, and receptive. You're a loyal and kind friend, always ready to help.

Magical Gifts: Goofy bestows the gifts of faithfulness, resiliency, and joy. He encourages you to have a positive attitude and not take yourself too seriously.

Keys to Your Success: Maintaining your zest for life.

Goofy's Story: *Mickey's Amateurs* (1937)

ROSIE You can handle the ups and downs of life; as a result, you are never down for long. Your positive attitude and compassion for those in pain are some of your greatest attributes. Successful and daring, you attempt feats that amaze others. You're creative and possess a candid sense of humor. "The show must go on" is your motto.

Magical Gifts: Rosie brings the gifts of caring, sensitivity, and the ability to tame the beastly side of others. Whenever you feel you've lost your nerve, ask her to show you her high-wire act.

Keys to Your Success: Making others' owies go away.

Rosie's Story: *A Bug's Life* (1998)

ACTIVE
CONFIDENT
EASY-GOING

FAWN You like to be outdoors and engage in physical activities. You have a talent for working with animals and are sympathetic to their needs. Working a job where you can have fun is vital to your well-being. You're a natural prankster and enjoy adventures. Clever and creative, you bring joy to everything you do.

Magical Gifts: Fawn bestows the gifts of enthusiasm, mischievousness, and an aptitude for languages. If your situation calls for rough-and-tumble playfulness, invite Fawn to help with the games.

Keys to Your Success: Hatching butterflies or assisting with any other kind of metamorphoses.

Fawn's Story: *Tinker Bell* (2008)

TUCK AND ROLL You use your body as a vehicle for self-expression. Physical power, beauty, and vocal ability are all possible talents. You have an uncomplicated sense of humor, and you're not offended if you're the only one who gets your jokes. Life, in your opinion, is meant to be enjoyed, and you prefer naughty over nice.

Magical Gifts: Tuck and Roll offer a magnetic personality, an agile body, and a desire to experience different cultures. When you have difficulty understanding what others are saying, they suggest nodding your head while remaining focused on your craft.

Keys to Your Success: Conveying your enthusiasm through applause.

Tuck and Roll's Story: *A Bug's Life* (1998)

WORLDLY
JOVIAL
COMMUNICATIVE

CLOPIN You share your insights with a wide audience. Because you have had many varied experiences, you easily see through the facades of others and perceive their underlying intentions. However, you too are mischievous and like to surround yourself in an air of mystery. You aren't afraid to stir the passions of your audience to make a statement. You possess leadership abilities and fiercely defend those under your care.

Magical Gifts: Clopin bestows the gifts of artistic expression, intelligence, and cunning. Call on him to assist you in openly revealing injustices.

Keys to Your Success: Using your creative abilities to inspire new ways of thinking.

Clopin's Story: *The Hunchback of Notre Dame* (1996)

POWERFUL
EXCEPTIONAL
AESTHETIC

GEORGETTE You possess star quality and work meticulously to perform the duties of your role. You are perceptive and notice everything and everyone in your surroundings. Knowing what people find appealing, you have the talent and ingenuity to produce it. You are straightforward, proud, and self-assured in your interactions. Yes, you do have a tender side, and only those clever enough to appreciate it win your heart.

Magical Gifts: Georgette gives the gifts of championship, sophistication, and creativity. She shows you how to confidently take your place among the winners.

Keys to Your Success: Inviting others into your life.

Georgette's Story: *Oliver & Company* (1988)

PRACTICAL
PATIENT
IDEALISTIC

GEORGE AND MARY DARLING

You strive to balance your responsible and romantic tendencies. You have a definite image of what it means to be mature, but it's hard for you to live up to it. Because you identify with the innocence of youth, you try to protect yourself and others from disillusionment. But it's your compassion (not your resolve) that is your strength and ultimately brings you closer to others.

Magical Gifts: George and Mary give the gifts of inspiration, sensitivity, and determination. Call on them when you wish to manifest a cherished dream.

Keys to Your Success: Keeping your imagination alive.

George and Mary's Story: *Peter Pan* (1953)

NALA You are tender and fierce. Most of the time, you just like to have fun with your friends. But in dire situations, you become brave. If you have no alternative, you will journey to unknown places to help those you love. Smart and sensible, you are able to convince others that by doing what's best for them, they are also doing what's best for the group.

Magical Gifts: Nala gives you the gifts of strength, good judgment, and intelligence. Summon Nala in times when you need clarity and compassion.

Keys to Your Success: Helping to boost morale.

Nala's Story: *The Lion King* (1994)

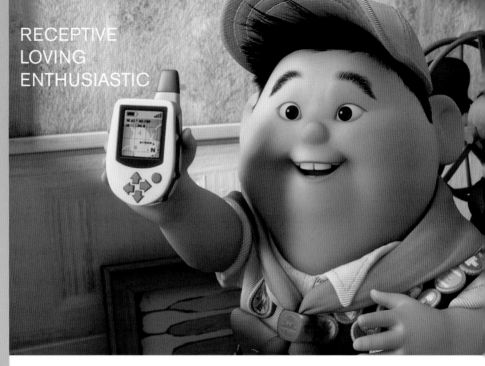

RECEPTIVE
LOVING
ENTHUSIASTIC

RUSSELL You love learning and sharing your expertise. You seek the company of others and are cheerful. When you want something, you go after it persistently and optimistically. Because you focus on the goal and not the details of the situation, you end up on some unbelievable excursions. You're an invaluable friend, and your services improve the lives of many.

Magical Gifts: Russell bestows the gifts of a warm heart, a love of animals, and a taste for adventure. He will teach you the skills needed for success.

Keys to Your Success: Doing what it takes to rise to the next level.

Russell's Story: *Up* (2009)

PRINCE PHILLIP You are a romantic. Guided by your heart, you place love above duty. You boldly pursue your ambitions, even if they're unpopular or challenge traditional expectations. Sometimes your quests take unplanned turns, but help always magically arrives just in the nick of time. Because you believe in you, others believe in you too. You have a playful sense of humor and are kind to animals.

Magical Gifts: Phillip bestows the gifts of cheerfulness, artistic expression, and vision. With his guidance, you can bring your fantasies to life.

Keys to Your Success: Slaying the dragon that keeps your dreams asleep.

Phillip's Story: *Sleeping Beauty* (1959)

DISTINCT
CREATIVE
GENEROUS

LOUIS You tend to have unusual interests and dreams that require persistence and ingenuity to accomplish. For that reason, you will travel far to achieve your goals. Nothing makes you happier than sharing your talents with those who appreciate them. Although you make a commanding first impression, your true nature is loving and gentle. You are a loyal and protective friend.

Magical Gifts: Louis bestows the gifts of passion, resourcefulness, and joy. He will help you develop your skills and figure out the best way to bring them into the world.

Keys to Your Success: Taking advantage of the opportunities all around.

Louis's Story: *The Princess and the Frog* (2009)

FAUNA You are artistic and enjoy experimenting with new ideas. Sometimes you take on the task of crafting grand projects before you've learned the basic techniques. You often let others take the lead, but you still express your individuality when performing your responsibilities. Charitable, you give people the benefit of the doubt. You are a loving and kind role model.

Magical Gifts: Fauna gives you the gift of song, creativity, and perception. When you need comfort and inspiration, choose something green to wear to welcome Fauna's magic.

Keys to Your Success: Working with your peers to ward off evildoers.

Fauna's Story: *Sleeping Beauty* (1959)

MUSICAL
EXPRESSIVE
OUTSPOKEN

ALLAN-A-DALE You are a chronicler. Many of the tales you tell convey a moral or spiritual message and immortalize past heroes and heroines. Then again, some of your stories are personal accounts of what you witnessed firsthand. Spreading your message through art, music, or the written or spoken word, you present controversial ideas to the public. You are poetic, romantic, and political.

Magical Gifts: Allan-a-Dale gives you the gift of voice. He teaches you to express your outlook in a way that educates and entertains others.

Keys to Your Success: Making sure your observations are genuine.

Allan-a-Dale's Story: *Robin Hood* (1973)

BERLIOZ You refuse to be left behind. You push yourself hard to keep up with and impress others. Clever and direct, you don't fall for people's antics. You like playful fighting because you envision yourself needing these skills in the future. (At least that's what you tell others.) Creative endeavors engage your mind and give you another means to release extra energy.

Magical Gifts: Berlioz gives you the gifts of confidence, intelligence, and musical abilities. He believes you should practice all the things you are good at to ensure your success.

Keys to Your Success: Developing your strength through positive channels.

Berlioz's Story: *The Aristocats* (1970)

FAIR
COMPASSIONATE
WISE

GRAND COUNCILWOMAN Your rational abilities allow you to rise to positions of authority. You remain calm in a crisis and carefully delegate responsibilities to the most capable people. Even though you have strong opinions, you will listen to advice. Well-intentioned, you give others a chance to reconcile their actions to achieve a common goal. Kind, serious, and perceptive, you want what's best for everyone.

Magical Gifts: Grand Councilwoman bestows the gifts of decisiveness, conscientiousness, and power. She guides you to use good judgment and understanding in every situation.

Keys to Your Success: Watching over families throughout our galaxy.

Grand Councilwoman's Story: *Lilo & Stitch* (2002)

ROGER RADCLIFFE You spend the early part of your life developing your talents. You often choose artistic careers that require you to work on your own. The solitude is great for inspiration, but it leaves you feeling lonely. Fortunately, there are others around you who prod you out of the house and have your romantic interests at heart. Once you make room in your life for love, you share a home filled with delightful and affectionate muses.

Magical Gifts: Roger gives you the gifts of creative ability and determination. Together, they assure your success.

Keys to Your Success: Knowing that dogs truly are people's best friends.

Roger's Story: *101 Dalmatians* (1961)

OPTIMISTIC
ORIGINAL
FEARLESS

ORVILLE You are a risk-taker—although to you, it doesn't feel like risk. You think of it as a step in getting to your preferred destination. Failure isn't in your vocabulary; you just don't view the world that way. You don't worry about what might happen; you just deal with problems when they arise. No one's sure exactly how, but somehow you always manage to avert trouble.

Magical Gifts: Orville brings the gifts of adventure, confidence, and spiritedness. He encourages you to keep trying until you're satisfied with the results.

Keys to Your Success: Landing safely on your feet.

Orville's Story: *The Rescuers* (1977)

FLIT You feel the most comfortable following an established path. Even so, you often align yourself with those who do just the opposite. When your friends embark on daring adventures, you go along, watching over and encouraging them to be careful. But it doesn't matter where you are; you lift the spirits of others just by being yourself.

Magical Gifts: Flit offers you the gifts of swiftness, joy, and a respect for tradition. When you're curious about what lies ahead, call on Flit to check it out for you.

Keys to Your Success: Protecting the natural order of life.

Flit's Story: *Pocahontas* (1995)

MAY 30

**QUICK-THINKING
CONFIDENT
SPONTANEOUS**

WILBUR Your inquisitiveness takes you on all kinds of escapades. Since you're not fond of rules or limitations, you take chances, believing in your ability to come out on top. You are strong-willed and prone to exaggerate the truth if it will help you achieve your goals. Your loved ones provide structure, keep you grounded, and give you the necessary tools for success.

Magical Gifts: Wilbur brings you the gifts of cleverness, daring, and accountability. Whenever your future is at stake, he'll help you retrace your steps and improve your outcome.

Keys to Your Success: Using time to your advantage.

Wilbur's Story: *Meet the Robinsons* (2007)

ARCHIMEDES You value reason. Practical, knowledgeable, and reserved, some of your closest friends are just the opposite. Although you do consider other points of view, you rarely embrace them. It's hard to get you to admit verbally that you care for someone, but your actions give you away. In fact, you can be protective and courageous when it comes to the well-being of loved ones.

Magical Gifts: Archimedes brings the gifts of intelligence, a good memory, and perception. He is ready to help you learn the skills necessary to become a benevolent sovereign.

Keys to Your Success: Mentoring those who touch your heart.

Archimedes's Story: *The Sword in the Stone* (1963)

CLEVER
ENCHANTING
SUPPORTIVE

GYPSY You know how to dazzle others with your visual appearance. You've learned the secrets of creating illusions, and you keep that information to yourself. Intelligent and insightful, you aren't upset by the frenzied actions of others. You perform your duties calmly and effortlessly. Ingenious and brave, you apply your specialized talents to varied situations. Your presence alone makes others shine.

Magical Gifts: Gypsy bestows the gifts of mystery, loyalty, and practicality. She teaches you the transformational quality of artistic expression, especially through color.

Keys to Your Success: Keeping your fans coming back for more.

Gypsy's Story: *A Bug's Life* (1998)

THE WHITE RABBIT You're always on the go. You definitely believe in multitasking; because of your eye for detail, your environment distracts you. A perfectionist by nature, you can't possibly fix everything that's not working, but you try. You are a sensitive, kind individual who selflessly tends to the needs of others. Whenever you show up, you get things moving forward.

Magical Gifts: The White Rabbit bestows the gifts of examination, gentleness, and thoughtfulness. When you want to visit someplace new and are in a hurry, just follow him.

Keys to Your Success: Knowing what time it is.

The White Rabbit's Story: *Alice in Wonderland* (1951)

ENTHUSIASTIC
CARING
PERSUASIVE

DORY You are very smart. But you're also absent-minded and easily lose focus when something new grabs your attention. You love to talk to others and explore ideas. Friendly and optimistic, you are eager to help people even if you don't know exactly how. Once you've satisfied your curiosity in your current surroundings, you come through swimmingly.

Magical Gifts: It's best to ask Dory what gifts you'd like from her, and write them down in a language she speaks. She'll get them for you and tell you a few funny stories too.

Keys to Your Success: Remembering details when it really counts.

Dory's Story: *Finding Nemo* (2003)

TERRANCE You are thoughtful and insightful, possessing deep wisdom of the heart. Certain objects appeal to you, and you're fond of collecting things. You like to have fun, and your daily life is full of activity. Those in your community count on your services and appreciate your attention to detail. Even though you choose to work in prominent professions, you don't take yourself too seriously.

Magical Gifts: Terrance brings the gifts of technical expertise, kindness, and intuition. Ask for his guidance whenever you need some extra sparkle to get the job done.

Keys to Your Success: Sharing your resources equitably.

Terrance's Story: *Tinker Bell* (2008)

UNCONVENTIONAL
CERTAIN
VISIONARY

MERLIN You rely heavily on intellect. Because you want to experience what you envision, you put yourself in diverse situations where you can stretch your perceptions and gain a deeper understanding of the world. You can be overly optimistic in thinking that brainpower can solve any problem and sometimes get yourself in precarious predicaments. But you also can get yourself out of them and are wiser from the journey.

Magical Gifts: Merlin bestows the gifts of magic, intelligence, and experimentation. With his guidance, you will see the possibilities that already exist in the future.

Keys to Your Success: Keeping your mind in the present.

Merlin's Story: *The Sword in the Stone* (1963)

RAFIKI Your contribution to society is to guide people toward their destiny. Your powers of perception are exceptional; even though you have great ability, you are humble and frequently downright silly. Versed in traditional wisdom, you use both unconventional and straightforward methods to awaken people to the errors of their thinking. Friends value your loyalty and leadership. You are a creative and amusing storyteller.

Magical Gifts: Rafiki gives you the gifts of friendship, spirituality, and humor. Seek his guidance when you are searching to understand your purpose in life.

Keys to Your Success: Becoming the trickster to enlighten others.

Rafiki's Story: *The Lion King* (1994)

POPULAR
MAGNETIC
HIGH-SPIRITED

MIA AND TIA You have enough energy for two people. Busy, busy, busy, you love to be where the excitement is. Getting swept away by the passion of the moment is not uncommon, and you idolize those who radiate charm and daring. You like to be part of the winning team, but your devotion is to the person and not to their chosen field of expertise. Your enthusiasm attracts your own group of admirers.

Magical Gifts: Mia and Tia bestow the gifts of optimism, style, and an appreciation for honorable champions. They show you how to have more fun.

Keys to Your Success: Enjoying the thrill of the race.

Mia and Tia's Story: *Cars* (2006)

ZINI You want others to notice and appreciate your unique qualities. Possessing an air of self-confidence, you are not shy about proclaiming your expertise. You are resourceful and wait for the right circumstances to guarantee your success. Most of all, you have a big heart and move out of your comfort zone to share your love with another.

Magical Gifts: Zini gives you the gifts of warmth, wit, and thoughtfulness. If you are unsure of how a situation will turn out, he'll give you lots of advice on how to proceed.

Keys to Your Success: Asking for help and liking it.

Zini's Story: *Dinosaur* (2000)

JUNE 9

RESILIENT
DETERMINED
EXCITABLE

DONALD DUCK You start out each day with a cheery outlook. But you quickly become annoyed when your everyday life doesn't live up to your standards. It isn't hard to tell what you're feeling since your emotions are plentiful, and you express them freely. Yet, you are persistent and never give up on yourself or your ambitions. Mischievous, outspoken, and helpful, you are entertaining and your behaviors endear you to others.

Magical Gifts: Donald bestows the gifts of tenacity, sensitivity, and authenticity. With his help, you can handle whatever comes your way, and give it all you've got.

Keys to Your Success: Having a joyful heart.

Donald's Story: *The Wise Little Hen* (1934)

ENERGETIC
CAUTIOUS
SASSY

JUNE 10

JESSIE You experience the fullness of life. Because you're intelligent, you use the wisdom you've gained from your encounters when making decisions about your future. You have a kind and cheerful disposition, and these qualities are most evident when you're part of a group or family. Talented in many areas, you simply must share your creativity with the world.

Magical Gifts: Jessie gives you the gifts of optimism, sensitivity, and agility. She'll help you ride through all the changes in life and remain safe and sound.

Keys to Your Success: Trusting the caring gestures of others.

Jessie's Story: *Toy Story 2* (1999)

INVENTIVE
ENCOURAGING
KNOWLEDGEABLE

MR. SOIL You hold a respected position in your community. Smart, artistic, and decisive, you have a variety of skills to choose from and develop. You prefer to have autonomy in your work and choose professions in which you can express yourself intellectually and creatively. People seek your counsel, and you remain composed and reassuring in situations that others find stressful.

Magical Gifts: Mr. Soil brings the gifts of leadership, influence, and learning. When something blocks your path, he will show you the best way around it.

Keys to Your Success: Helping those less experienced than you succeed.

Mr. Soil's Story: *A Bug's Life* (1998)

MARAHUTE You are both powerful and gentle. You appreciate the kindness of others and are committed to your family and friends. Generous and playful, you lovingly share your possessions with loved ones. You're patient and tenacious, remaining optimistic even in difficult situations. Those closest to you protect you and make sacrifices to ensure your lasting freedom. Your genuineness and intimacy soften the hearts of others.

Magical Gifts: Marahute brings the gifts of compassion, distinctiveness, and wisdom. She will fly down and comfort you whenever you feel disconnected from nature.

Keys to Your Success: Knowing that others will come to your aid when you need it most.

Marahute's Story: *The Rescuers Down Under* (1990)

SELF-ASSURED ADVENTUROUS & FEARLESS

PETER PAN You have an active fantasy life. You love stories that take you to fairytale lands populated by heroes, villains, and magic. Mundane work drains your vitality. When you bring your outstanding creative skills to an intellectual project or product, you excel. However, when you use your ingenuity solely for daydreaming, you forfeit your life to the fleeting pleasures of escapism.

Magical Gifts: Peter gives you the gifts of youthfulness, mischievousness, and leadership. When you need inspiration, he will help you recall the wonder and magic of childhood.

Keys to Your Success: Finding a place to live that supports your dreams.

Peter's Story: *Peter Pan* (1953)

FOXY LOXY You have abundant energy and lots to say. You're forceful; people definitely know when you're in the room. You have talent but tend to take it for granted. Learning comes easily, and you don't always realize that is a strength not everyone possesses or can develop. In time, your competitive spirit wanes, and you become interested in forming intimate friendships.

Magical Gifts: Foxy likes gifts; she brings you intelligence, courage, and alien transformations. Call on her when you need help developing the right heroic attitude.

Keys to Your Success: Enjoying the benefits of getting your brainwaves scrambled.

Foxy's Story: *Chicken Little* (2005)

ASSURED
SUAVE
WARM

PRINCE NAVEEN You are fun-loving and clever. It's easy for you to convince people to follow your wishes; when they do, you often underestimate the consequences of your actions. But you're not afraid of new experiences and make the best out of every endeavor. You win the hearts of others through your charm and gregariousness.

Magical Gifts: Prince Naveen bestows the gifts of optimism, spiritedness, and adaptability. With his guidance, you will take an amazing journey to discover what is important to you.

Keys to Your Success: Realizing that a little effort brings you love and fulfillment.

Prince Naveen's Story: *The Princess and the Frog* (2009)

JOCK You plan for the future. To you, security is vital, and you always have something discreetly set aside in case you need it later. When it comes to your friends, you generously give of yourself if it benefits their happiness. You are insightful and careful not to say anything that would cause a loved one to feel bad or inferior.

Magical Gifts: Jock brings the gifts of honesty, practicality, and compassion. He will tell you the truth about any situation and unselfishly help you find solutions.

Keys to Your Success: Being a good friend.

Jock's Story: *Lady and the Tramp* (1955)

DEPENDABLE
COMMANDING
TRUTH-SEEKING

CHIEF POWHATAN You are proud of your place in society. You take your family and work responsibilities seriously. Many of your decisions come from the traditions and spiritual beliefs of those who raised you. You rely on those values to direct your life, but you will listen to opposing ideas from people you love, trust, and respect. You're powerful and protective, and no one can ignore your presence or influence.

Magical Gifts: Chief Powhatan imparts the gifts of leadership, spirituality, and sentiment. Call on his guidance when you need support making life-changing decisions.

Keys to Your Success: Honoring your choices, wherever they lead.

Chief Powhatan's Story: *Pocahontas* (1995)

DOC You take the lead in matters of home and work. When worried, you have difficulty expressing yourself but manage to get your meaning across. Your role in the family is much like that of an elder, and you enjoy advising those you care about. If someone needs your help, they can count on you to sacrifice your own comfort on their behalf.

Magical Gifts: Doc bestows the gifts of headship, empathy, and a love of music. He helps you make sensible decisions at significant life moments.

Keys to Your Success: Leading others to the diamond mines.

Doc's Story: *Snow White and the Seven Dwarfs* (1937)

SPIRITED
AMBITIOUS
BRAVE

PRINCESS DOT You need to express yourself and hate limits of any kind. Because you're convinced that you can do anything that your more experienced companions can do, you sometimes push yourself too hard. Still, you persist, and you encourage others in the beginning stages of learning something new to keep at it. Feisty, bright, and rebellious, you befriend those with innovative ideas.

Magical Gifts: Dot brings the gifts of determination, perception, and independence. She teaches you to question the world around you and come up with your own answers.

Keys to Your Success: Inspiring others to believe in themselves.

Dot's Story: *A Bug's Life* (1998)

B.E.N. You are friendly and unique. You don't like being alone for long periods, so companionship is an essential component to your happiness. You have technical talents that are advantageous, and others recognize them before you do. Fiercely loyal and eager to please, you thrive when you can work as part of a team and help your friends.

Magical Gifts: B.E.N. bestows the gifts of optimism, tenacity, and excitement. Whenever you feel distraught, ask him to help you recover the missing parts of yourself that will make you whole again.

Keys to Your Success: Being with people who value your company.

B.E.N.'s Story: *Treasure Planet* (2002)

MISCHIEVOUS
AWARE
ENCHANTING

TINKER BELL You have your own special brand of magic. People admire your spirit and your playful and sometimes naughty nature. You thrive when you're the center of attention; but when you're not, your pouting makes your displeasure known. Because you form strong emotional bonds, you are protective and do your best to guard those you care about.

Magical Gifts: Tinker Bell bestows the gifts of ingenuity, joy, and hope. Whenever you need swift help getting yourself and others out of harm's way, she'll sprinkle you with pixie dust.

Keys to Your Success: Lighting up the nighttime sky.

Tinker Bell's Story: *Peter Pan* (1953)

BASHFUL You are in love with love and the adventure it promises. Idealistic, you are capable of great emotion. Since you don't like to draw attention to yourself, the object of your affections may never know your true feelings. Still, you can be a bit of a flirt and are a sucker for love songs, love stories, and basically anything that has to do with love and the wishes tucked inside your heart.

Magical Gifts: Bashful bestows the gifts of aesthetics, imagination, and adoration. He quietly advises you to follow your dreams, even if they make you blush.

Keys to Your Success: Using your modesty to your advantage.

Bashful's Story: *Snow White and the Seven Dwarfs* (1937)

GENUINE
AFFECTIONATE
EAGER

DUG Your life excites you, and your propensity for fun distracts you from what you're supposed to be doing. Although at first glance you appear average, once people get to know you they discover that you have some incredible abilities. Loyal, trusting, and kind, you assume that everybody's motivations are as sincere as your own. Happily, you align yourself with those who wholeheartedly love and care for you.

Magical Gifts: Dug brings you the gifts of charisma, enthusiasm, and expressiveness. He encourages you to confidently say what you're thinking and feeling.

Keys to Your Success: Doing plenty of what comes naturally to you.

Dug's Story: *Up* (2009)

THE FAIRY GODMOTHER You are adept at your profession. You're able to look at mundane items in your environment and devise clever uses for them. Sympathetic to the plights of others, you devote your talents to helping them rise above their circumstances. Your imagination and warm heart enhance the lives of young people and children and provide them with the tools needed to ensure their happiness.

Magical Gifts: The Fairy Godmother bestows the gift of manifestation and the sensibility to use it wisely. Under her guidance, the impossible becomes possible and rewarding.

Keys to Your Success: Making dreams come true with a wave of your wand.

The Fairy Godmother's Story: *Cinderella* **(1950)**

NURTURING
PLAYFUL
GENEROUS

KANGA You devote yourself to what is most important to you, whether family, work, or self. You love to take care of people, solve problems, and give thoughtful advice. In your home, you prefer things to be clean and organized. Intuitive, you always seem to know the right action to take, which impresses others. It doesn't matter if someone is family or friend; you treat them both with equal compassion.

Magical Gifts: Kanga gives you the gifts of observation, a warm heart, and a gentle disposition. Call on her when you need comfort and nurturing.

Keys to Your Success: Caring for those in your neighborhood.

Kanga's Story: *Winnie the Pooh and the Honey Tree* (1966)

MR. INCREDIBLE (aka Bob Parr)
You are happiest when providing a crucial service to society. Mundane work zaps the life from you, so you want to save the world to save yourself from boredom. Your love of adventure can get you into situations that are more than you imagined. You don't readily ask for help, but thankfully your loved ones are always by your side.

Magical Gifts: Mr. Incredible bestows the gifts of determination, sensitivity, and humanitarianism. When you find yourself living in the past, he will show you what you're missing in the present.

Keys to Your Success: Discovering the power of working with others.

Mr. Incredible's Story: *The Incredibles* (2004)

PERSISTENT
CONSIDERATE
GENTLE

OLIVER You are affectionate, loyal, and brave. You quickly learn what it takes to triumph in your environment. Adaptable and clever, you're never one to start a fight, but you're a fierce competitor when provoked. Sympathetic to the heartaches of the people you love, your presence heals their loneliness. Your friends come from all walks of life, and you feel equally at home with each of them.

Magical Gifts: Oliver bestows the gifts of deep emotions, perseverance, and teamwork. Together, you can heal the hearts of those who need you as much as you need them.

Keys to Your Success: Going after what is rightfully yours.

Oliver's Story: *Oliver & Company* (1988)

FUNNY
LOVING
UNCOMPLICATED

MATER You are friendly and like to tease people in a caring way. When someone is in trouble, you're the first one at the scene. Your gentle, playful demeanor puts others at ease. Because you have such a big heart, you attract acquaintances who want to repay your kindness by helping you fulfill your dreams. Not one to obsess over your appearance, you love yourself as you are.

Magical Gifts: Mater bestows the gifts of humor, charm, and special skills. He encourages you to enjoy the simple things in life.

Keys to Your Success: Seeing the potential for goodness in all your new best friends.

Mater's Story: *Cars* (2006)

**SENSITIVE
CAUTIOUS
INSPIRED**

MICHAEL DARLING You have a kind disposition and take careful risks. When you explore something unknown, you want the company and security of trusted people by your side so you can develop your talents naturally. You tend to follow more than lead, and you can get lost in the adventures of others. Nevertheless, each exploit feeds your creativity and teaches you something new.

Magical Gifts: Michael brings you the gifts of playfulness, virtue, and daring. He shows you how to bring your dreams to life by keeping one foot in reality at all times.

Keys to Your Success: Making sure you never forget where you came from.

Michael's Story: *Peter Pan* (1953)

INDUSTRIOUS
PERCEPTIVE
THOUGHTFUL

EUDORA You are an entrepreneur. You're good with details and can translate ideas into form. Hardworking and nurturing, you devote as much energy to your loved ones as you do to your work. You have a practical imagination, and you inspire people to dream big and to discover what is truly important to them. Understanding and tolerant, you treat others with compassion and respect.

Magical Gifts: Eudora bestows the gifts of kindness, ingenuity, and conscientiousness. She encourages you to cultivate your creativity and find happiness in everything you do.

Keys to Your Success: Using your artistic talents to bring joy to others.

Eudora's Story: *The Princess and the Frog* (2009)

PERCEPTIVE
SENTIMENTAL
EMOTIONAL

RUNT OF THE LITTER You are concerned with living up to the expectations you've set for yourself. You admire family members and want to be like them. Although having positive role models to emulate helps you, it also causes you to overlook the unique qualities in yourself that are worth developing. Luckily, you have loyal and empathetic friends who understand and feel the same way as you.

Magical Gifts: Runt bestows the gifts of devotion, belonging, and love. If you need protection, he will courageously come to your aid.

Keys to Your Success: Listening to soothing music.

Runt's Story: *Chicken Little* (2005)

THE DRAGON You pursue pastimes that make you happy. It's easy for you to make friends, and your original way of existing in the world piques the interest of others. Although you prefer to be your natural self, when you do take on a role, you are an exciting entertainer. You have many talents and may be the first in your family to display them.

Magical Gifts: The Dragon bestows the gifts of imagination, magic, and refinement. He reminds you that you have the power to decide if someone is a friend or foe.

Keys to Your Success: Staying true to who you are.

The Dragon's Story: *The Reluctant Dragon* (1941)

WISE
ATTENTIVE
PERSUASIVE

BIG MAMA You are sensitive to the emotional pain endured by others. You do more than lift their spirits, you make sure they are cared for and provide an environment where they can thrive. Honest and observant, you help those in your care and do your best to ensure their happiness before sending them on their way.

Magical Gifts: Big Mama bestows the gifts of guidance, understanding, and optimism. In times of despair, let her show you where to look to see the beauty in your life.

Keys to Your Success: Fostering others until they can make it on their own.

Big Mama's Story: *The Fox and the Hound* (1981)

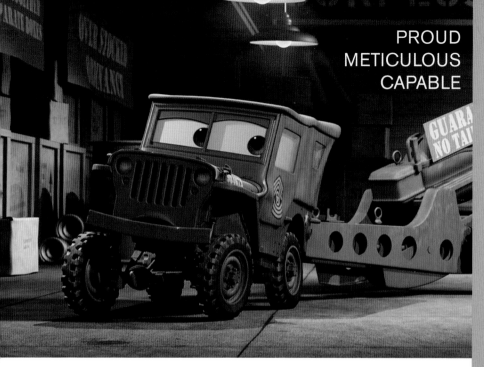

SARGE You are concerned about your home, family, and community. You acquire a sense of pride when safeguarding and guiding others. A perfectionist, you believe there is a right way of doing things. Hidden beneath your need for precision and commitment to duty is a kind, loving, and devoted individual who will do anything for the ones you love.

Magical Gifts: Sarge bestows the gifts of bravery, compassion, and faithfulness. If you need help getting the job done, he will motivate you with his tales of heroism and a few off-road calisthenics.

Keys to Your Success: Admitting you enjoy the company of those who can drive you crazy.

Sarge's Story: *Cars* (2006)

IMAGINATIVE
RESPECTFUL
LOVING

ANDY You enjoy inventing and demonstrating your ideas. People provide you with the toys you need to bring your fantasies to life. Your loved ones look up to you, and you are considerate and fun to be around. When you're busy, the time you spend with them is limited. Even though you like new things, you still love what you already have.

Magical Gifts: Andy bestows the gifts of curiosity, enthusiasm, and loyalty. He encourages you to use your creative talents to make those you care about feel special.

Keys to Your Success: Filling your space with items that inspire you.

Andy's Story: *Toy Story* (1995)

PERDITA You follow the needs of your heart when making important decisions. You are perceptive and know instinctively how someone feels about you. You're capable of supervising large projects or groups of people, and others feel contented in your care. Although you're a worrier, once you commit yourself to a cause, you stick with it. Gentle and accepting, you attract those who can benefit most from your compassion.

Magical Gifts: Perdita gives you the gifts of devotion, kindheartedness, and wisdom. She will provide the energy and support needed to meet your most treasured obligations.

Keys to Your Success: Making room in your life for everyone who needs you.

Perdita's Story: *101 Dalmatians* (1961)

INTUITIVE
NURTURING
COMMUNICATIVE

WENDY You are highly aware of the world around you. Some of what you see you don't like, and as a result you head in the opposite direction. Once you release your idealized image of how you should conduct yourself and start being you, others will come around to your point of view. You're creative, brave, and caring, and loved ones benefit from your insight.

Magical Gifts: Wendy gives you the gifts of honesty, intelligence, and vision. She encourages you not to grow up so quickly that you overlook the magic all around.

Keys to Your Success: Believing until your dreams come true.

Wendy's Story: *Peter Pan* (1953)

DJANGO You are protective of those you love. You prefer established methods to achieve success. It takes a while for you to warm to new ideas, especially if they challenge your own. You're hard to impress unless you can see the benefits of an endeavor. Your willfulness results from your love and devotion to family and friends. Beneath your no-nonsense exterior lies a heart of gold.

Magical Gifts: Django brings you the gifts of leadership, sensibility, and sincerity. He will share his knowledge of the world and ensure your safety.

Keys to Your Success: Respecting the choices of loved ones.

Django's Story: *Ratatouille* (2007)

JULY 9

EXPRESSIVE
GENEROUS
LOVING

GEPPETTO You focus your imagination on producing things that give others great joy. You are not materially driven. Instead, you perfect your craft for the pleasure and satisfaction it brings you. Because much of your artistic work is solitary, you form strong attachments to the finished product. Many of your creations become people's prized possessions. You are kind and nurturing toward animals and people who need your guidance and attention.

Magical Gifts: Geppetto bestows the gifts of craftsmanship, dedication, and compassion. He teaches you to ask the universe to help make your dreams come true.

Keys to Your Success: Bringing your dreams to life.

Geppetto's Story: *Pinocchio* (1940)

PIGLET Your home is important to you, and it's where you express yourself fully. You treasure the intimacy of close relationships. Friendship is especially precious because it provides you with the support and motivation you need to be courageous. A devoted friend, you will give up your own comfort to help another.

Magical Gifts: Piglet bestows the gifts of gentleness, sacrifice, and intellect. He encourages you to discover the strength that is deep inside you and call upon it whenever you want to try something new.

Keys to Your Success: Having a cozy home filled with everything you love.

Piglet's Story: *Winnie the Pooh and the Blustery Day* (1968)

ENTHUSIASTIC
HEADSTRONG
IMAGINATIVE

CHARLOTTE LA BOUFF You know exactly what you want from an early age and are determined to reach your goal. Stories of love and prominence inspire you. You're in a hurry to create the future that you picture in your mind. There are a few special people you form close relationships with, and as you mature, your devotion to them deepens. A visual person, you gravitate toward beautiful surroundings and belongings.

Magical Gifts: Charlotte bestows the gifts of persuasion, opportunity, and creativity. She will help you realize your most valued dreams.

Keys to Your Success: Discovering that friendship is what makes you truly wealthy.

Charlotte's Story: *The Princess and the Frog* (2009)

RAJAH You look out for those you love. Committed to friends and family, you love people with all your heart and actively seek their company. Because you don't want your loved ones to be in pain, you support the wishes of others even when they differ from your own. Clever and playful, you have a strong physical presence and use it to manage others without ever needing to say a word.

Magical Gifts: Rajah bestows the gifts of mischievousness, tenderness, and friendship. He will scare away anyone who tries to keep you from achieving your destiny.

Keys to Your Success: Consoling others with the strength of your love.

Rajah's Story: *Aladdin* (1992)

AFFECTIONATE
COURAGEOUS
LUCKY

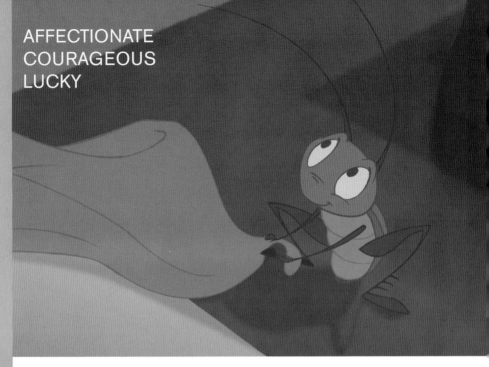

CRI-KEE You are loving and dutiful. Because people believe in your abilities, you have high expectations for yourself. You are sensitive and care deeply for those who depend on you. Although at times you can be cautious and uncertain, when in the midst of an adventure you are bold and accomplish heroic feats. You're playful and intelligent, and others feel better just having you around.

Magical Gifts: Cri-Kee bestows the gifts of conscientiousness, determination, and empathy. He will keep you safe and comfort you on all your journeys.

Keys to Your Success: Sticking by others until they discover their good fortune.

Cri-Kee's Story: *Mulan* (1998)

OWL You are eager to share what you know. Tales of your ancestry fascinate you and make you proud. You're not overly concerned about the accuracy of your stories; in fact, sometimes you're not even aware that what you're saying may not be entirely true. For you, the enjoyment is in the performance and captivating your audience. When you express yourself through words and writing, you have a unique command of the English language.

Magical Gifts: Owl's gifts are wisdom, creativity, and consideration. He teaches you to explore the deeper meaning of things.

Keys to Your Success: Sharing stories that entertain.

Owl's Story: *Winnie the Pooh and the Honey Tree* (1966)

AESTHETIC
GENTLE
STEADFAST

FERDINAND THE BULL You appreciate the beauty found in nature and the physical world. You travel at your own pace, and it's almost impossible to make you change direction once you form an attachment to something. Your peaceful disposition attracts others to you and allows you to live your life on your own terms. On the rare occasion when you do get upset, you express your discomfort clearly and then move on.

Magical Gifts: Ferdinand bestows the gifts of serenity, originality, and focus. He reminds you to choose your own destiny and not to fear letting others see who you really are.

Keys to Your Success: Devoting your time to doing what you love most.

Ferdinand's Story: *Ferdinand the Bull* (1938)

PRINCE ERIC You are a dreamer. If something catches your eye that resembles your heart's desire, you immediately go after it. You're quite capable of making what you want happen as long as you don't get sidetracked and lose sight of what you originally wanted. Although you're strong and protective, you will accept the help of others when you need it.

Magical Gifts: Prince Eric bestows the gift of profound love for partner, family, animals, and the sea. He encourages you to pursue, with bravery and determination, the vocation that calls to you.

Keys to Your Success: Finding the one you're looking for.

Prince Eric's Story: *The Little Mermaid* (1989)

RITA You are self-reliant and resourceful. Friendly and kind to newcomers, you understand their apprehension and make them feel welcome. Sharing what you know with others, you let them decide the best plan for their lives. You are content with the life you carved out for yourself and the people you share it with. Clever and strong, you have a style that suits you perfectly.

Magical Gifts: Rita bestows the gifts of respect, capability, and awareness. She will teach you the necessary skills to live successfully in a big city.

Keys to Your Success: Having a heart of gold.

Rita's Story: *Oliver & Company* (1988)

DALLBEN You possess a powerful insight into the affairs of the world. You are empathetic and have a profound knowledge that goes beyond learning. Because you understand the responsibility that comes with this state of awareness, you carefully mentor those with similar abilities. You often worry about the safety of others, placing their welfare above your own. Courageous and kind, you side with the forces of good.

Magical Gifts: Dallben bestows the gifts of wisdom, humbleness, and mystery. He will provide you with the essential knowledge required for you to begin your life's journey.

Keys to Your Success: Sheltering those whose powers are rare.

Dallben's Story: *The Black Cauldron* (1985)

SENSITIVE
DIRECT
ARTISTIC

FRANCIS Your masculine and feminine qualities are equally strong. You are heroic and emotional, aggressive and maternal, all at the same time. It upsets you when others get the wrong impression of you. Your close friends see the real you, and you love to banter with them. Even though you try to deny it, you love the task of nurturing others.

Magical Gifts: Francis gives you the gifts of courage, wit, and tenderness. He supports you in your quest to reveal your talents to the greatest audience you can find.

Keys to Your Success: Enjoying the company of those who adore you.

Francis's Story: *A Bug's Life* (1998)

SUPERNATURAL
AMUSING
ETHICAL

THE GENIE You live in both the invisible and visible worlds. You understand the power of thoughts, energy, and intentions and know how they shape reality. Experiences that could be unnerving to some, you move through with humor and courage. Your talents are impressive, and you develop them to the highest degree. You can work wonders for the sake of others, and often do. Ultimately, you persuade others to merely be themselves.

Magical Gifts: The Genie bestows the gifts of responsibility, perception, and exuberance. He teaches you about the accountability that comes with making and granting wishes.

Keys to Your Success: Using your powers to liberate yourself.

The Genie's Story: *Aladdin* (1992)

OBSERVANT
PASSIONATE
ENDURING

MICHAEL "GOOB" YAGOOBIAN You are receptive to people and circumstances in your environment. You do your best to accommodate the needs of others, even if it means compromising your own success. When you don't have to compete and can enjoy your favorite pastimes, you feel blissful. Following your innate wisdom is the key to your fulfillment.

Magical Gifts: Goob brings the gifts of discernment, humbleness, and fortitude. If you are feeling bad about a situation, he will guide you to listen to the positive advice offered by others and discard the negative.

Keys to Your Success: Knowing you always have a choice in creating your future.

Goob's Story: *Meet the Robinsons* (2007)

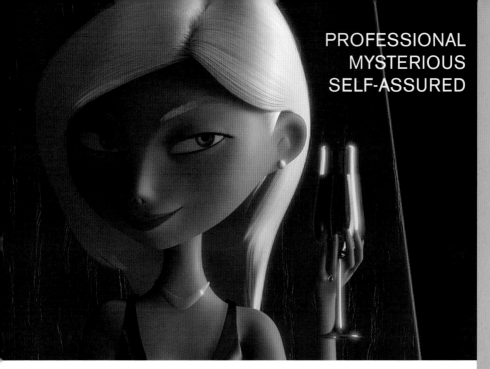

MIRAGE You dedicate yourself to doing a good job. You are caring, thorough, and intelligent. You're sharp and know what makes people tick, and you use that information to persuade them to do what you want. In relationships, you are idealistic and can misread the intentions of loved ones. But once you see the truth, you quickly change course and make the right decisions for your future happiness.

Magical Gifts: Mirage bestows the gifts of confidence, allure, and awareness. She will help expose illusions before they cause harm.

Keys to Your Success: Working with people who genuinely care about you.

Mirage's Story: *The Incredibles* (2004)

BOLD
TRUSTING
INDEPENDENT

PATCH You long to know what makes you special. This yearning causes you to explore places where you feel more distinct. You choose heroes and heroines who reflect your desire to possess talents no one else has and memorize every detail about them. This helps you develop your own talents. Before long, you come to the happy realization that you are special, and always were.

Magical Gifts: Patch bestows the gifts of intelligence, inquisitiveness, and self-awareness. He teaches you to value and cultivate your authentic qualities instead of revering the pretend abilities in someone else.

Keys to Your Success: Feeling good about yourself and your place in your family.

Patch's Story: *101 Dalmatians II: Patch's London Adventure* (2003)

FLOUNDER You enjoy spending time with friends and will follow them into uncharted waters. Sometimes you get anxious when exploring unfamiliar places, but you act bravely anyway. Intuitive, you sense things before they happen. You are unwavering in your support of those you care about, and when they need you, you're there. Your confidence and certainty strengthen over time.

Magical Gifts: Flounder bestows the gifts of companionship, resourcefulness, and charisma. Call on him when you need a friend to stick by your side through thick and thin.

Keys to Your Success: Learning when to stay behind and when to follow.

Flounder's Story: *The Little Mermaid* (1989)

LOVEABLE
DECISIVE
EXUBERANT

LUIGI You are pleased with who you are and where you come from. Your distinct tastes reveal the best of what your culture has to offer. Foreign places excite you, and you like to have a few good friends along to share in the experience. Filled with enthusiasm for life, you possess an amusing, childlike wonder that attracts people to you.

Magical Gifts: Luigi bestows the gifts of optimism, spontaneity, and a heart filled with tears of joy. He believes you should proudly tell everybody that you have what they want.

Keys to Your Success: Knowing what your favorite things are.

Luigi's Story: *Cars* (2006)

COURAGEOUS
TENACIOUS
GOOD-HUMORED

MOWGLI You feel at home in nature and have an exceptional bond with animals. You prefer to do things your own way and at your pace. With your magnetic personality, making friends comes easily; but your agreeable nature sometimes makes you too trusting. Wise beyond your years, you have a lot to offer your family and community. Animals willingly befriend, nurture, and protect you.

Magical Gifts: Mowgli bestows the gifts of confidence, playfulness, and adaptability. He teaches you how to create a home in many different environments.

Keys to Your Success: Listening to advice and accepting when it's time to move forward.

Mowgli's Story: *The Jungle Book* (1967)

GENUINE
STRONG
THOUGHTFUL

MULAN You make tough choices that affect your future place in society. You try your best to play the roles offered to you, but your personality is too powerful to be contained. Although you are respectful of and loving to those you care about, ultimately you must be true to yourself. You are intelligent, considerate, and full of life. Whatever you set out to achieve, you accomplish with dignity.

Magical Gifts: Mulan bestows the gifts of heroism, ingenuity, and devotion. When you're required to make a difficult decision, she will guide you to the admirable choice.

Keys to Your Success: Seeing your immeasurable worth every time you look in the mirror.

Mulan's Story: *Mulan* (1998)

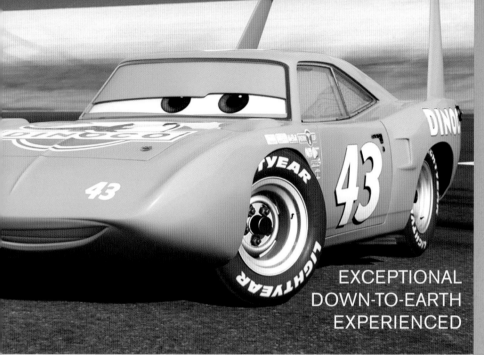

**EXCEPTIONAL
DOWN-TO-EARTH
EXPERIENCED**

THE KING You are focused and hard-working. You benefit from the support and sacrifices of the people closest to you. Admired and respected for your lifelong achievements, you know that your notoriety is the result of teamwork. In fact, it is the dedication of the group that you treasure most. Because you know what's most important for your happiness, you prioritize your commitments accordingly.

Magical Gifts: The King gives you gifts of opportunity, determination, and the thrill of victory. Call on him when you want to make sure your championship cup is overflowing.

Keys to Your Success: Enjoying the ride for as long as you want.

The King's Story: *Cars* (2006)

PERCEPTIVE
SPIRITED
NURTURING

CHICHA You live your life according to your values. You have the energy to handle numerous responsibilities in a thoughtful manner. Smart and clever, you see the slippery intentions of others and skillfully beat them at their own game. You believe that each person deserves respect and appreciation. Feisty, you communicate your thoughts and feelings directly with humor and love.

Magical Gifts: Chicha bestows the gifts of self-confidence, awareness, and capability. Call on her whenever you need encouragement and support to stand up for yourself and your family.

Keys to Your Success: Loving yourself, your family, and your life.

Chicha's Story: *The Emperor's New Groove* (2000)

ABU You are a loyal friend, and your friends bring out the best in you. You have lots of energy, and almost everything you see catches your interest. You keep yourself occupied by investigating your surroundings and meeting new people. You have manual dexterity and physical agility, which provide many practical capabilities that you put to excellent use. When circumstances warrant, you can be extremely generous.

Magical Gifts: Abu bestows the gifts of aptitude, humor, and companionship. Because you're good at so many things, he'll help you pick what to do first.

Keys to Your Success: Enjoying your favorite foods in the company of friends.

Abu's Story: *Aladdin* (1992)

PERCEPTIVE
UNDERSTATED
STRAIGHTFORWARD

BRIDGET You are self-aware and independent. You analyze your environment and notice the weaknesses. Pragmatic, you work cooperatively with others to remedy the situation. You value relationships, but only pursue those in which you are sincerely respected and valued. Sometimes you don't recognize your positive qualities and use humor to downplay them. You have a tough persona that lets others know you mean business; it earns you the admiration you desire.

Magical Gifts: Bridget brings you the gifts of elegance, perception, and common sense. She encourages you to stand tall and gracefully show your spots.

Keys to Your Success: Realizing that love is right under your nose.

Bridget's Story: *The Wild* (2006)

DODGER You are pleased with your abilities and who you are. You're a survivor and adept at acquiring what you need. Personal freedom is essential because you like to be your own boss. You are loyal and protective of those you love. When it comes to your accomplishments, you like to embellish your stories with acts of personal heroism. Dignified and influential, you are a lively leader.

Magical Gifts: Dodger gives the gifts of independence, fearlessness, and ingenuity. With his help, you'll have all the resources you need to succeed.

Keys to Your Success: Knowing there is no reason for you to worry.

Dodger's Story: *Oliver & Company* (1988)

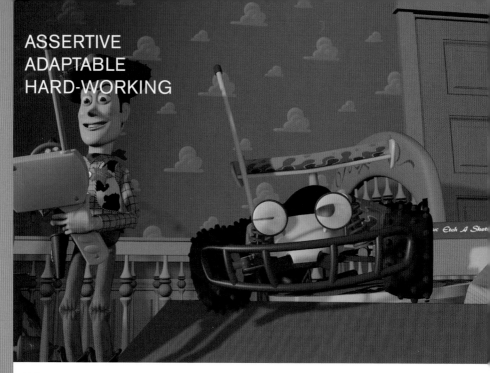

ASSERTIVE
ADAPTABLE
HARD-WORKING

RC Those closest to you know that your actions speak louder than words. You have a significant effect on the lives of others and give everything you have to important matters. Although you feel most confident when in charge of a situation, you will let those you care about take the lead when they need to. Sensitive to your environment and the people in it, your best friends help you to stay on track.

Magical Gifts: RC brings you the gifts of liveliness, direction, and resilience. He'll show you the fastest route to attaining your desires.

Keys to Your Success: Taking time to rest and recharge your batteries.

RC's Story: *Toy Story* (1995)

CAPTAIN PHOEBUS You live the life of adventure. Sympathetic to injustices endured by others, you are principled and fight for what you believe is right. Sure of yourself, you imagine victory but sometimes overestimate your capabilities. Fortunately, loved ones do their best to come to your aid. Romantic and flirtatious, you win the affections of the partner you desire.

Magical Gifts: Phoebus gives you the gifts of integrity, confidence, and wit. Whenever you find yourself in situations that require an extra dose of courage, he'll be there to assist you.

Keys to Your Success: Using your humor to lighten serious situations.

Phoebus's Story: *The Hunchback of Notre Dame* (1996)

ECCENTRIC
SINGLE-MINDED
CHARITABLE

MILO JAMES THATCH Your heritage inspires you, and you love to learn. In fact, once you get interested in something, it borders on an obsession. Although you have a strong mind, you're open to new ideas. When you discover the truth, you do what's required to resolve the situation, even if it causes you grief in the end. You shield those you love.

Magical Gifts: Milo gives you determination, compassion, and intelligence. With his assistance, you can leave the known for the unknown.

Keys to Your Success: Staying true to your aspirations no matter how unattainable they seem to others.

Milo's Story: *Atlantis: The Lost Empire* (2001)

CAPTAIN AMELIA You have a no-nonsense approach to life. You're witty and concise, always allowing others to know your opinion of them and the situation. Since you're capable of handling things on your own, it takes time for people to see your warm and nurturing qualities. Yet when someone does appeal to your softer side, you become a devoted and supportive partner.

Magical Gifts: Amelia gives you the gifts of leadership, poise, and discernment. Ask for her guidance when you need help deciding on the best course of action.

Keys to Your Success: Leading people to their buried treasures.

Amelia's Story: *Treasure Planet* (2002)

AFFECTIONATE
ADEPT
SUPPORTIVE

VIXEY You are strong and capable. You're open and friendly to others from different backgrounds and places. Your playful and spirited personality entices people to you. Although independent, you're happiest when you can share your life with loved ones who cherish and admire you. Smart, tender, and headstrong, you make a heartening friend and partner.

Magical Gifts: Vixey gives you the gifts of curiosity, intuition, and mystery. Whenever you feel abandoned or alone, she will accompany you and help you develop your survival skills.

Keys to Your Success: Guiding others with wisdom and love.

Vixey's Story: *The Fox and the Hound* (1981)

ALADDIN You have a romanticized image of who you want to be. As a result, you can talk yourself into doing things that are not always in your best interest. The paradox is that you are already the person you envision, and you have the power to awaken the riches that dwell inside you. You are caring, bright, and resourceful. Why would you wish to be anything else?

Magical Gifts: Aladdin bestows the gifts of bravery, cleverness, and self-discovery. He assures you that who you really are holds more happiness and fulfillment than your fantasies.

Keys to Your Success: Achieving your dreams without tricks.

Aladdin's Story: *Aladdin* (1992)

CLEVER
DARING
SPONTANEOUS

ROBIN HOOD You take on many disguises depending on which role you are attempting to portray. You have compassion for those less fortunate and will use whatever means available to provide for others. Although this is a noble deed, not everyone agrees with your methods for obtaining and redistributing resources. Because you enjoy challenging authority, you believe your actions are noble. You are loyal and lighthearted in your relationships.

Magical Gifts: Robin Hood bestows the gifts of imagination, optimism, and luck. He encourages you to find work that is fun and rewarding.

Keys to Your Success: Bringing hope and inspiration to others.

Robin Hood's Story: *Robin Hood* (1973)

PLIO You provide a strong, stable presence for those in your immediate environment. You are wise and experience life from a spiritual perspective. Through love and tenderness, you help others face their fears and insecurities. You are optimistic and have faith in people and the future. Confident, you can persuade others to follow your ideas. You are truthful and enlighten others on how their thoughts and actions influence their happiness.

Magical Gifts: Plio gives you the gifts of understanding, strength, and devotion. Call on her when you need guidance in adapting to new environments.

Keys to Your Success: Knowing that our time on earth is precious.

Plio's Story: *Dinosaur* (2000)

AUGUST 10

TALENTED
ENCHANTING
INTUITIVE

THE PRINCE You have a calm and powerful presence that impacts the lives of others. You express yourself artistically through singing, speaking, or both. Either way, the sound of your voice captivates. You follow your heart in most things, and your loved ones can always depend on you to be there. Setbacks don't discourage you from attaining your goals because you know just what to do to further things along.

Magical Gifts: The Prince bestows the gifts of patience, confidence, and sensitivity. Ask for his help when you want to awaken your dreams.

Keys to Your Success: Knowing when to show up.

The Prince's Story: *Snow White and the Seven Dwarfs* (1937)

TUG You have a talent for bringing people together. You not only share your own stories but also take a genuine interest in those of others. Respected and tolerant, you are an amicable leader. When you interact with people, your words are kind, playful, and encouraging. Because you're comfortable in your own skin, you put others at ease. You are perceptive and recognize the needs of those in your environment.

Magical Gifts: Tug bestows the gifts of acceptance, unconditional love, and guidance. When you're in an unfamiliar place, he will offer you an invitation to join the group.

Keys to Your Success: Establishing an inclusive sense of community.

Tug's Story: *Brother Bear* (2003)

AUGUST 12

TRADITIONAL
RESPONSIBLE
SUPPORTIVE

NAKOMA You are proud of your ancestry. You prefer the security found in established systems, and you encourage those dear to you to respect and consider the wisdom found in their teachings. Faithful, sensible, and empathetic, you are concerned for your family and friends and do what you can to ensure their happiness. You are serious in important matters, but also can be playful and loving.

Magical Gifts: Nakoma bestows the gifts of friendship, culture, and thoughtfulness. Call on her guidance when you're ready to begin walking your path.

Keys to Your Success: Knowing that we all have our own individual destinies to follow.

Nakoma's Story: *Pocahontas* (1995)

SKIPPY You are confident that you will make it no matter what obstacles come your way. Your optimism comes from experience because, like magic, help always appears from unexpected sources when you need it most. You idealize the accomplishments of unconventional individuals and work to support their efforts. Others may tease you in your initial attempts to achieve success, but you emerge victorious in the end.

Magical Gifts: Skippy gives you the gifts of skill, imagination, and gratitude. Whenever you think a situation is hopeless, he will provide the help and tools you need to triumph.

Keys to Your Success: Believing in your ability to prosper.

Skippy's Story: *Robin Hood* (1973)

**GENUINE
SENSITIVE
OBLIGING**

REX You are concerned about your place in society. Even though you are cared for and capable, you can let your fears and self-doubt get the best of you. With the help of supportive friends, you accomplish things you never thought possible. When you aren't trying so hard, you can be heroic. In the end, you realize that believing in yourself is all you have to do.

Magical Gifts: Rex bestows the gifts of honesty, tenderness, and strength. When you feel frightened, ask him to help you uncover your dinosaur power.

Keys to Your Success: Knowing you did it and can continue doing it.

Rex's Story: *Toy Story* (1995)

THE BEAST You have a heart bursting with competing desires. Your mind can be an unreliable judge casting harsh determinations on your worth and that of others. You understand the power of love by experiencing the effects your actions have on others. Luckily, the beautiful essence of who you are never dies; in time it is liberated and allowed its full expression.

Magical Gifts: The Beast bestows the gifts of reflection, strength, and majesty. Call on him when you need help returning to your true nature.

Keys to Your Success: Allowing the one you love to come to you.

The Beast's Story: *The Beauty and the Beast* (1991)

AUGUST 16

CAPABLE
INTELLIGENT
OBSERVANT

EVE You focus on achieving your goals with fierce determination. You don't let others stand in the way of what you want, and you're used to being valued for your abilities versus who you are. However, you are not immune to the powers of love, and the genuine affection of another surprises and intrigues you. Once you apply your exceptional talents to your personal relationships, your life becomes more meaningful—and a lot more fun.

Magical Gifts: EVE brings you the gifts of strength, willpower, and sensitivity. She will guide you in the direction of your heart's desires.

Keys to Your Success: Making time for romance.

EVE's Story: *WALL•E* (2008)

KUZCO You like being in charge and are happy with your successes. You are strong-willed and learn best through experience. Sometimes you're unaware of the impact of your decisions on others. But when someone shows you kindness and acts unselfishly, you will place their wishes above your own. Exuberant and funny, you enjoy breaking the rules.

Magical Gifts: Kuzco loves gifts, and he will make sure one of his assistants brings you whatever you desire. When he's around, you'll experience the best that life has to offer.

Keys to Your Success: Using your position to improve the lives of others.

Kuzco's Story: *The Emperor's New Groove* (2000)

AUGUST 18

REFLECTIVE
COURAGEOUS
RESPONSIVE

SIMBA You are destined for greatness, but your path will not be easy. At times, you are carefree and enjoy a leisurely lifestyle. But if something unexpected happens, you tend to want to run away and forget. That is not your fate. Your ability to feel profound emotions and take responsibility for your actions makes you a wise and much-needed leader.

Magical Gifts: Simba gives you the gifts of wisdom, strength, and conscience. He encourages you to never shrink away from your destiny.

Keys to Your Success: Remembering who you were born to be.

Simba's Story: *The Lion King* (1994)

KEVIN You have a colorful personality. You are quirky, impulsive, and loving. Circumstances beyond your control can cause you to seclude yourself from the everyday world until it is safe to emerge. You are good at keeping secrets and protecting those under your care. With a select few, you come out of hiding and show your carefree and expressive side. Your sweet, gentle nature draws compassionate people into your life who will assist you.

Magical Gifts: Kevin gives you the gifts of feistiness, joy, and individuality. Call on her when you want to uncover your uncommon beauty.

Keys to Your Success: Preserving the qualities that make you special.

Kevin's Story: *Up* (2009)

INNOCENT
SERIOUS
DARING

BOLT Your life is a mystery waiting to be unraveled. Hidden in your past are untold stories of your origins. Sometimes they aren't literal secrets, but something you don't entirely understand about yourself. Either way, once you awaken to the truth about yourself and your true talents, your life changes dramatically for the better. You are happiest when you use your imagination to create something real and lasting.

Magical Gifts: Bolt bestows the gifts of compassion, artistic expression, and bravery. He helps you perceive yourself and the world as it truly is.

Keys to Your Success: Having people around who love you and think you are super-wonderful just for being you.

Bolt's Story: *Bolt* (2008)

CHRISTOPHER ROBIN You are a kind and compassionate person. You enjoy spending time celebrating successes with your close friends. A quiet and intelligent leader, you can quickly solve and mediate the problems of others. Once the crisis is resolved, you return to what you were doing. You're a good listener and provide honest, tender advice.

Magical Gifts: Christopher Robin gives you the gifts of imagination, virtue, and devotion. He reminds you how much those who share your everyday world appreciate you.

Keys to Your Success: Helping but not intruding into the lives of those you love.

Christopher Robin's Story: *Winnie the Pooh and the Honey Tree* (1966)

AUGUST 22

ENTHUSIASTIC
HARD-WORKING
INSPIRED

ELLIE You focus your energies on attaining future goals. You enjoy the journey of getting there as much as the ambitions you hope to achieve. When you meet someone new, you know instantly if you like them. Once you form a friendship, you are loyal and include your new friend in cherished pursuits. You are spontaneous, compassionate, and fond of children and animals.

Magical Gifts: Ellie brings the gifts of appreciation, wisdom, and spiritedness. She encourages you to write down all your experiences so that you remember your blessings and share them with others.

Keys to Your Success: Knowing that dreams come true in ways you hadn't originally imagined.

Ellie's Story: *Up* (2009)

BASIL OF BAKER STREET You are shrewd and good at solving mysteries. Your thoughts excite you, and you are happiest when quickly figuring out a complex problem. When you run into obstacles, you become disheartened. Having others around to assist and point out things you overlooked lifts your spirits. Although you do care for others, you don't always verbally convey the depth of your feelings.

Magical Gifts: Basil gives you the gifts of reason, imagination, and expertise. He shows you how to use the power of your mind to help those in trouble.

Keys to Your Success: Outsmarting your opponents.

Basil's Story: *The Great Mouse Detective* (1986)

CERTAIN INVESTIGATIVE PRINCIPLED

AGENT WENDY PLEAKLEY You are a highly unique individual. Depending on where you live, you may or may not fit in. The farther away from home you go, the more you stand out. This makes you nervous because you like to survey your surroundings inconspicuously. You learn quickly, but can jump to conclusions before collecting all the facts. In all situations, you are concerned with doing what is ethically correct.

Magical Gifts: Pleakley gives you the gifts of enthusiasm, inquisitiveness, and a love of knowledge. Ask for his support when you're exploring unknown places.

Keys to Your Success: Knowing that you're beautiful.

Pleakley's Story: *Lilo & Stitch* (2002)

ROSETTA You have a sharp mind and seek perfection in everything you do. Well mannered, you don't like poor hygiene or sloppiness. You are encouraging and love to counsel others. Sassy, stubborn, and wise, you bring confidence and expertise to whatever you do. You love color, art, and nature. Attuned to your senses, you surround yourself with pleasing scents, sights, and sounds.

Magical Gifts: Rosetta bestows the gifts of gardening, charm, and insight. When you need to look your best, she will provide you with her best tips and tricks guaranteed to impress.

Keys to Your Success: Using your artistic abilities to make the world lovelier.

Rosetta's Story: *Tinker Bell* (2008)

AUGUST 26

RESERVED
ANALYTICAL
SUPPORTIVE

DOCTOR DOPPLER You are aware of your abilities and know what you can and cannot do. You are imaginative, long for adventure, and spend years perfecting your craft. Perceptive and spontaneous, you don't censor your thoughts and can say something inadvertently. Your main goal is to be helpful to others. You choose strong, dynamic partners who appreciate your knowledge and assistance.

Magical Gifts: Doctor Doppler gives you the gifts of technical knowledge, assets, and companionship. Call on him to supply the courage to seize an opportunity that allows you to pursue your dreams.

Keys to Your Success: Asserting your desires in any environment.

Doctor Doppler's Story: *Treasure Planet* (2002)

MRS. POTTS You are friendly, resilient, and supportive. You make every effort to create a positive environment for those you care about, no matter what the circumstances. Although you benefit from serving others, sometimes the situations you find yourself in take years to transform. Still, you refuse to give up on your dreams and work hard to provide the resources needed for success.

Magical Gifts: Mrs. Potts bestows the gifts of understanding, idealism, and intuition. In the midst of chaos, she shows you how to have an inspiring and soothing influence on others.

Keys to Your Success: Helping people prevail over difficult enchantments.

Mrs. Potts's Story: *Beauty and the Beast* (1991)

HONEST
OBSERVANT
ENCOURAGING

THUMPER You are a communicator. You notice all the details in the world around you. When you discover something new, you like to share it with everyone. Caring, enthusiastic, and helpful, you do your best to assist your companions. You are a playful teacher and try hard to understand the needs of others. Physical activities are a perfect outlet for you to release excess nervous energy.

Magical Gifts: Thumper brings the gifts of intelligence, courage, and friendship. He teaches you how to overcome your fears by scaring them away.

Keys to Your Success: Knowing when it's better not to say anything at all.

Thumper's Story: *Bambi* (1942)

JAMES HENRY TROTTER You are a gentle soul. You are wise and possess an inner radiance that no one can diminish. At times the world around you seems harsh, but you are cooperative and find nonaggressive ways to handle the situation. Humane, you befriend and protect the tiniest inhabitants in nature. Those closest to you hold you in the highest esteem, and it is well deserved, for you are an extraordinary person.

Magical Gifts: James bestows the gifts of grace, imagination, and compassion. Under his tender guidance, your sense of self will survive and thrive.

Keys to Your Success: Remembering what fun is for.

James's Story: *James and the Giant Peach* (1996)

SOCIABLE
RESPONSIBLE
INFLUENTIAL

ELI "BIG DADDY" LABOUFF You are optimistic and self-assured. You are good with money and shower those you care about with attention and gifts. Although you hold an important and powerful role in society, you have a big heart and are a pushover for loved ones. In your business dealings, you are gracious and fair. You enjoy hosting grand events and making sure everyone has a good time.

Magical Gifts: Big Daddy brings you the gifts of prosperity, generosity, and caring. Whenever you need help funding your dreams, call on him to help you acquire the necessary resources.

Keys to Your Success: Using your position to enhance the lives of others.

Big Daddy's Story: *The Princess and the Frog* (2009)

ZAZU You take your obligations seriously and fulfill numerous functions. You follow the rules of the game and grow frustrated when things don't go as planned. Proud, proper, and dignified, you don't get upset when others tease you. Instead, you use humor to get your point across, bringing a smile to their faces. You are aware of all that's going on around you and make an excellent advisor.

Magical Gifts: Zazu gives you the gifts of observation, faithfulness, and intelligence. Call on him when you need an update on your current situation.

Keys to Your Success: Entertaining others with your superb wit.

Zazu's Story: *The Lion King* (1994)

ENERGETIC
INTELLIGENT
ENTERPRISING

CHIP You focus your brilliant mind on achieving what you desire—and you desire a lot. Confident that you can attain what you want, you lead others toward that common goal. Ever serious about the task at hand, you cleverly scan your surroundings for advantageous opportunities. You grow impatient when others clown around but easily forgive those you care about, because you know they make your life much more fun.

Magical Gifts: Chip brings you the gifts of logic, determination, and mischievousness. He can help you find a solution to any problem.

Keys to Your Success: Appreciating the talents of your friends.

Chip's Story: *Toy Tinkers* (1949)

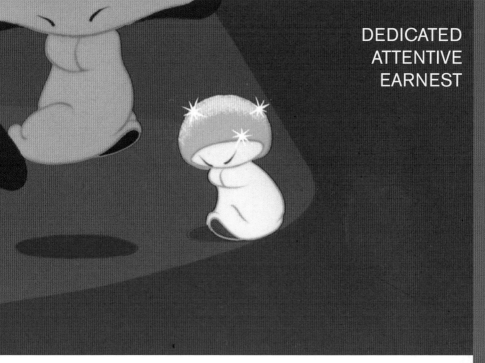

HOP LOW Your showmanship emerges at a young age. Before your talents are fully developed, your achievements already captivate others. You seek out older and accomplished mentors to help develop your skills. Focused, you work diligently at becoming proficient in your trade, knowing exactly where you need to improve and what you must master to succeed. Others respect your efforts and surround you with positive reinforcement.

Magical Gifts: Hop Low bestows the gifts of patience, aptitude, and physical agility. With his help, you can reach your goals and take your place at center stage.

Keys to Your Success: Finding your own rhythm.

Hop Low's Story: *Fantasia* (1940)

SEPTEMBER 3

SACRIFICING
ENDURING
DEEP

NITA You are unafraid to walk a different path. Only your insecurities can hold you back, but those who love you help vanquish them. You don't reveal the motivations behind your actions, yet the depth of your emotions powers them. The partners you choose are the ones you can have fun with. You are loyal, honor your commitments, and are kindhearted to all earth's creatures.

Magical Gifts: Nita bestows the gifts of devotion, tenderness, and courage. Through her guidance, you reclaim latent talents and find your home in the world.

Keys to Your Success: Letting love transform you.

Nita's Story: *Brother Bear 2* (2006)

BERNARD People notice your potential before you do. You start out humbly, performing mundane tasks, but sooner or later achieve greatness. Because you're thorough in your work and concerned about the welfare of others, people specifically request your assistance. Although you tend to worry about the future, romance brings out your courage and your will to prevail. Fireworks fill the sky when you're with the one you love.

Magical Gifts: Bernard gives you the gifts of intelligence, capability, and magnetism. He is there to help whether your request is big or small.

Keys to Your Success: Knowing that your actions do make a difference.

Bernard's Story: *The Rescuers* (1977)

IMAGINATIVE
HELPFUL
ENDEARING

SCUTTLE You are creative and like to share your musings with others. Your curiosity takes you on various adventures. You want to figure things out, and you'll come up with your own explanations if unable to find definitive information. This talent allows you to fly above everyday problems and come up with inventive solutions. You care about others, and they can count on you in times of crisis.

Magical Gifts: Scuttle gives you the gifts of optimism, warmth, and expertise. He will fancifully teach you everything you want to know about mysterious artifacts.

Keys to Your Success: Getting the facts straight in important matters.

Scuttle's Story: *The Little Mermaid* (1989)

CINDERELLA You gracefully handle whatever life has to offer. Although your circumstances may change drastically, you remain constant, and any hardship you do encounter only makes you more beautiful. You look for the good in everyone, but if someone bullies you, you stand up for yourself and clearly state your desires. Gracious, you are grateful for the things your friends do for you. You love animals and adore their companionship.

Magical Gifts: Cinderella gives you gifts of determination, imagination, and faith. She encourages you to ask for guidance when you need it and trust that it will appear.

Keys to Your Success: Letting destiny work its magic.

Cinderella's Story: *Cinderella* (1950)

PRACTICAL
DISCIPLINED
CARING

SIR ECTOR You focus on obtaining a specific goal. Methodical and in charge, you believe success is a result of obedience and practice. Although you make your decisions based on reason, you are sympathetic to the needs of others. You are the first to apologize if you have misjudged someone. Once the workday is done, you are warm, relaxed, and witty.

Magical Gifts: Sir Ector bestows the gifts of observation, responsibility, and benevolence. He offers you the guidance and essentials needed to fulfill your destiny.

Keys to Your Success: Providing a secure home fit for a future king or queen.

Sir Ector's Story: *The Sword in the Stone* (1963)

SULTAN You try hard to balance the needs of your loved ones with the demands of society. You rely on conventional wisdom when making decisions and have honorable intentions. As an honest person, you are surprised when others try to deceive you. Above all, you want people to be happy, and you do what you can to ensure a pleasant outcome. You carefully deliberate opposing views and then make progressive decisions that benefit others.

Magical Gifts: Sultan bestows the gifts of prosperity, power, and kindness. He encourages you to rule by following the needs of your heart.

Keys to Your Success: Respecting the wishes of others.

Sultan's Story: *Aladdin* (1992)

SEPTEMBER 9

ENDEARING
HUMBLE
PERSEVERING

LINGUINI Your ultimate success comes from your ability to keep moving forward no matter the odds. It takes a while for you to discover where you fit in the world, and you try different things until you find the right people and circumstances to help you thrive. You work best as part of a team and admire the wisdom of others. Your friends provide you with invaluable assistance in attaining your goals.

Magical Gifts: Linguini bestows the gifts of sincerity, cooperation, and tenderness. Call on him when your task requires inspiration and precision.

Keys to Your Success: Amassing knowledge from a variety of experts.

Linguini's Story: *Ratatouille* (2007)

DEDICATED
KIND
INTELLIGENT

SEPTEMBER 10

WALL•E You take on enormous responsibilities with ease. Not one to complain, you focus on the job at hand, often working in solitude. You like to accrue things and understand how they work. Humble and shy, you observe others before revealing yourself. Hopelessly romantic and idealistic, you follow the yearnings of your heart, waiting to share yourself and your special treasures with your beloved.

Magical Gifts: WALL•E gives you the gifts of curiosity, renewal, and optimism. He reminds you that each of us has the power to shape the world's future.

Keys to Your Success: Faithfully doing your work because you know it has potential value.

WALL-E's Story: *WALL•E* (2008)

ALERT
DUTIFUL
SENSITIVE

COPPER You make important decisions in your life that affect the well-being of those closest to you. As a loyal person, you become confused when the people you're loyal to are in conflict with one another. You learn through experience and are able to move beyond what others taught you to believe to live your life according to what is true for you.

Magical Gifts: Copper gives you the gifts of friendship, maturity, and listening to the wisdom of your heart. Under his guidance, your friends will never turn into enemies.

Keys to Your Success: Choosing strategies in which no one gets hurt.

Copper's Story: *The Fox and the Hound* (1981)

GILL You are imaginative and view life from many perspectives. You yearn for freedom and encourage and empower people to embark on daring adventures. Never one to be down for long, you continually devise elaborate strategies aimed at benefiting the lives of everyone around you. You are mysterious, love ceremony, and act in accordance with your beliefs. Friends depend on your insight and direction in tough situations.

Magical Gifts: Gill bestows the gifts of bravery, determination, and leadership. He inspires you to keep up your spirits and let your dreams propel you onward.

Keys to Your Success: Helping others find their way back home.

Gill's Story: *Finding Nemo* (2003)

LOVEABLE
APPRECIATIVE
COURAGEOUS

WHEEZY You hold a special place in the lives of many people. Forever ready to share the song in your heart with loved ones, you have an uncanny ability to show up at the perfect time. Your friends would do anything for you, and you feel the same allegiance toward them. At times you appear shy, but you really sparkle when able to reveal your talents to a select crowd.

Magical Gifts: Wheezy gives you the gifts of perseverance, healing, and understanding. When you need a reminder to believe in yourself, call on him to lift your spirits.

Keys to Your Success: Finding your voice.

Wheezy's Story: *Toy Story* (1995)

RABBIT You keep track of what goes on in your environment. You solve problems using your intellectual skills, and you're proud of your reasoning ability. Meticulous, you like things just so and have little patience for those who act impulsively and don't prepare for the future. Nonetheless, you are a loving, thoughtful friend who will tolerate the imperfections of others and help them succeed.

Magical Gifts: Rabbit brings you the gifts of compassion, observation, and intellect. Whenever life gets messy, ask him to straighten out the muddle so you can go have fun.

Keys to Your Success: Leading others on exciting explorations.

Rabbit's Story: *Winnie the Pooh and the Honey Tree* (1966)

GENTLE
OPTIMISTIC
HEROIC

QUASIMODO You work hard to find your place in society. Sensitive and idealistic, you regularly seek refuge in your safe haven to rejuvenate and shield yourself from the demands of everyday life. A visual person, you have considerable artistic abilities. Once people get to know you, they find a warm, loving, and intelligent being with much to contribute. You are a loyal and altruistic friend.

Magical Gifts: Quasimodo bestows the gifts of creativity, observation, and tenacity. Whenever you feel confined by your circumstances, ask him for the guidance you need to set yourself free.

Keys to Your Success: Becoming your own master.

Quasimodo's Story: *The Hunchback of Notre Dame* (1996)

JOHN DARLING You are spirited and ready to test the limits of your ideas. You are bright and focus your thoughts on attaining success. Taking great pride in your appointed position, you take your responsibilities seriously and perform them confidently. All that duty and obligation gets tiresome, however, and you soon find yourself engaging in more playful pastimes. On the inside, your true aspiration is to enjoy life on your own terms and live it at your own pace.

Magical Gifts: John bestows the gifts of daring, creativity, and youthfulness. With his guidance, you'll explore worlds you never knew existed.

Keys to Your Success: Letting your imagination fly.

John's Story: *Peter Pan* (1953)

SEPTEMBER 17

SERVICE-ORIENTED
ASTUTE
DILIGENT

DR. FLORA You are dependable and take an active role in society. Knowledgeable and just, you choose positions in which you can positively influence the lives of others. Your responsible nature comforts those who rely on your services. You don't use your mind purely for practical pursuits, however; you are also creative and connected to the earth's energy. When not working, you like to get out and listen to music.

Magical Gifts: Flora bestows the gifts of benevolence, leadership, and wisdom. Call on her counsel when you're learning about nature's medicinal qualities.

Keys to Your Success: Keeping those in your care fit and healthy.

Flora's Story: *A Bug's Life* (1998)

HONEST
ENIGMATIC
MATTER-OF-FACT

RICK DICKER You tend to be a private person and excel at handling confidential information. Because of your ability to get things done in a proficient and sensible manner, your talents are highly respected and sought after by important people. Empathetic and protective toward your friends, you will tackle difficult circumstances to ensure their safety. You are a realist with a soft heart and never give up on causes you believe in.

Magical Gifts: Rick gives you the gifts of reliability, concentration, and discretion. He reminds you that even superheroes need the help of trusted friends.

Keys to Your Success: Using your skills to mediate extraordinary situations.

Rick's Story: *The Incredibles* (2004)

ELEGANT
CULTURED
NURTURING

DUCHESS You take great care in the image you present to others. You desire harmonious environments and encourage loved ones to be respectable, polite, and well-mannered. Those close to you sometimes challenge your idealistic view of the world, but at the same time they respect your success. Though you enjoy material comforts, the happiness and well-being of your family and friends are what matter to you most.

Magical Gifts: Duchess gives you aesthetic abilities, sound judgment, and social skills. When you want to make a striking impression, she will help you look and perform your best.

Keys to Your Success: Enriching the lives of others through love and loyalty.

Duchess's Story: *The Aristocats* (1970)

SALLY You know that appearance alone doesn't guarantee happiness. You have diverse talents and may engage in more than one profession. Socially conscious, you use your skills to improve the lives of others. You are determined and fight for what you believe is worth renovating and revitalizing. Playful, smart, and perceptive, you like to spend time relaxing and getting to know people.

Magical Gifts: Sally brings the gifts of intelligence, responsibility, and wisdom. Whenever you feel empty inside, she encourages you to give yourself the space to let something new emerge.

Keys to Your Success: Knowing when it's time to change course.

Sally's Story: *Cars* (2006)

ECCENTRIC
CLEVER
EXCITABLE

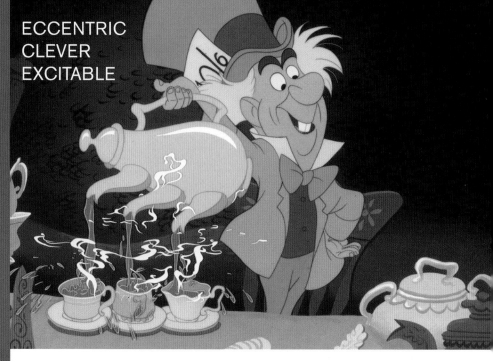

MAD HATTER You are physically expressive. You enjoy taking everyday objects and experiences and tweaking them into something new. This can backfire when you're helping those who don't appreciate your creative abilities. Because you love to play with ideas, you can be ineffective in practical matters. Like-minded friends encourage your outrageousness and partake in your zany endeavors.

Magical Gifts: Mad Hatter bestows the gifts of imagination, companionship, and originality. He shows you how to see the world from a different perspective and use it to your advantage.

Keys to Your Success: Playing with time, and whatever else you can get away with.

Mad Hatter's Story: *Alice in Wonderland* (1951)

TIMON You like to live in places where you have a lot of freedom and not many cares. But that doesn't mean you want to be alone. You like hanging out with friends, bantering, and getting plenty of attention. Insightful, you understand the behaviors of others. When it comes to the special people in your life, you are accommodating, protective, and ready to lend a hand in their success.

Magical Gifts: Timon bestows the gifts of self-confidence, cleverness, and helpfulness. If you're traveling to new lands, call on him as a guide to adventure and fun.

Keys to Your Success: Having no worries.

Timon's Story: *The Lion King* (1994)

RESOLUTE
BRIGHT
SPONTANEOUS

PRINCESS JASMINE You are determined to realize your ambitions and won't let anyone stand in your way. You were born with many advantages that can feel like disadvantages when you're operating out of duty. Attuned to aesthetics, you love beautiful things; but they don't entrance you. You are independent and remain unaffected by others' attempts to change you. When it comes to romance, anything less than true love won't do.

Magical Gifts: Jasmine bestows the gifts of courage, intelligence, and strength. She encourages you to be a free spirit and to think for yourself.

Keys to Your Success: Challenging outdated traditions that limit your freedom.

Jasmine's Story: *Aladdin* (1992)

RAY You follow your heart wherever it leads you. Others don't always understand your longings, but their doubts never dissuade you from your dreams. You're driven by a higher form of love, and your ideals carry you far. Your positive nature lifts the spirits of everyone around you and inspires them to believe in themselves. Gentle and wise, you help others open their hearts and find lasting happiness.

Magical Gifts: Ray brings the gifts of warmth, optimism, and imagination. He encourages you to utilize the power of love to make your wishes come true.

Keys to Your Success: Following the glimmer inside your heart.

Ray's Story: *The Princess and the Frog* (2009)

SEPTEMBER 25

WISE
APPROACHABLE
DEVOTED

QUEEN CLARION You are concerned with the welfare of others. You have a peaceful approach to life and a well-established method of teaching and guiding those in your environment. Discord and chaos upset you, and you can sometimes value harmony above the truth in situations. Responsible, encouraging, and kind, you don't take yourself too seriously, which is your greatest wisdom.

Magical Gifts: Queen Clarion bestows the gifts of adeptness, endurance, and prosperity. She will help you discover your unique talent and provide the resources needed to develop it.

Keys to Your Success: Considering the knowledge gained from starting new traditions.

Queen Clarion's Story: *Tinker Bell* (2008)

ROZ You believe there is a right way and a wrong way to do things. You have formulated a method that allowed you to achieve considerable success, and you implement it with wit and precision. Others aren't always privy to your personal life or past, but they can count on you to make wise and compassionate decisions that reflect your empathy and heart.

Magical Gifts: Roz brings you the gifts of perception, mystery, and influence. Call on her when you need to uncover the truth regarding a situation and thoughtfully conceal the facts.

Keys to Your Success: Holding every key to every door.

Roz's Story: *Monsters, Inc.* (2001)

SUPPORTIVE
FOCUSED
CAPABLE

BEAVER You put all your efforts into achieving a specific goal. Your work tends to be solitary, but when others cross your path, you receive unexpected rewards from the encounter. You're honest and friendly, so strangers feel comfortable asking you for assistance, which you willingly offer. You're humble, sensible, and extremely talented in your chosen vocation.

Magical Gifts: Beaver brings the gifts of determination, success, and trust. Ask for his help whenever the obstacle you are facing requires strength and expertise to remove.

Keys to Your Success: Discovering that when you help others, your life gets easier.

Beaver's Story: *Lady and the Tramp* (1955)

MEGARA You are romantic but also realistic. Much of your life experience revolves around your relationships and the choices you make to sustain them. Even though you're partnership-oriented, you remain self-sufficient. You can be sharp witted, especially when protecting yourself from potential disappointment. No matter how difficult the circumstances, you have the courage and ingenuity to achieve your desires.

Magical Gifts: Megara bestows the gifts of resourcefulness, confidence, and devotion. Ask for her guidance when you have to make tough decisions concerning your future happiness.

Keys to Your Success: Opting for sacrifices that will enrich your life.

Megara's Story: *Hercules* (1997)

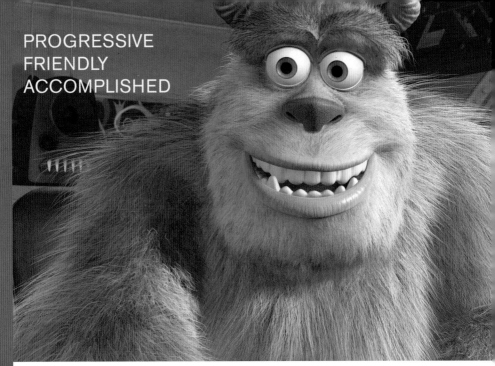

PROGRESSIVE
FRIENDLY
ACCOMPLISHED

SULLEY You have natural talents that allow you to rise to the top of your field. Work excites you, and you enjoy friendly competition as long as everyone plays fair. Loyal and modest, you don't mind helping people succeed in your same line of work. You have a laid-back attitude about most things, but when someone touches your heart, you will sacrifice everything to care for them.

Magical Gifts: Sulley gives you the gifts of sincerity, insight, and devotion. He will help you determine when the time is right to make your own rules.

Keys to Your Success: Discovering that laughter increases your energy.

Sulley's Story: *Monsters, Inc.* (2001)

SUSIE You have a beautiful smile that attracts others. You interact with people from all walks of life and gain valuable life experience. Accepting of but not always comfortable with your present situation, you have the resolve to hold out until the atmosphere changes in your favor. It's important that you take excellent care of yourself, because your well-being increases your self-confidence and helps maintain your youthful appearance.

Magical Gifts: Susie gives you the gifts of longevity, expressiveness, and love. She reminds you to have faith in your future destiny.

Keys to Your Success: Having the opportunity to rebuild your life.

Susie's Story: *Susie, the Little Blue Coupe* (1952)

COLLABORATIVE
SOPHISTICATED
CONFIDENT

PONGO You take part in larger-than-life endeavors. Because of your generous and well-meaning intentions, what you attempt brings positive and lasting results. You work equally well alone or with others and frequently take the lead. However, sometimes the enormity of the task at hand requires the loving support of partners to keep you focused. You are playful, responsible, and proud of those you consider family.

Magical Gifts: Pongo gives you the gifts of caring, tenderness, and ingenuity. He shows you how to help others realize their dreams while creating your own.

Keys to Your Success: Being part of a supportive social network.

Pongo's Story: *101 Dalmatians* (1961)

HAMM You are a people watcher. You observe your surroundings and then publicly deliver your message with a mix of honesty and humor. Assured in your beliefs, you remain open to new information and act accordingly. You enjoy being part of a group, and when the opportunity arises you like to be in charge of a project. You are dedicated, intelligent, and appealing.

Magical Gifts: Hamm brings you the gifts of friendship, prosperity, and commitment. If you're unable to see what's happening outside your front door, ask Hamm to tell you the details.

Keys to Your Success: Holding on to your spare change.

Hamm's Story: *Toy Story* (1995)

ARTISTIC
CONFIDENT
WARM

BIANCA You are capable, focused, and optimistic. Because you have a big heart, you choose vocations in which you provide people with much-needed assistance. You are daring and love to conquer challenges. When you require the support of others to complete your missions, you have an uncanny ability to pick the perfect allies. Your loved ones are eager to impress and care for you.

Magical Gifts: Bianca bestows you with the gifts of knowledge, ability, and attractiveness. No matter where you are, if you need help, just send her a message.

Keys to Your Success: Bringing beauty and humanity bravely into the world.

Bianca's Story: *The Rescuers* (1977)

BUCK "ACE" CLUCK Your life offers you many out-of-the-ordinary experiences. You're a sincere person who relies on your established belief system to try to adapt to the unexpected. Because you're concerned about doing the right thing and protecting those you love from harm, you can misread the needs of others. But you're perceptive, and your devotion to family motivates you to move beyond your comfort zone.

Magical Gifts: Buck gives the gifts of guidance, talent, and responsibility. He teaches you to nurture others by believing in their dreams.

Keys to Your Success: Expressing your feelings openly to those you love.

Buck's Story: *Chicken Little* (2005)

OCTOBER 5

GENTLE
RESPECTFUL
HEROIC

ALADAR You are a survivor. Your presence is both powerful and tender. Because you are brave and loyal to the people and causes you believe in, and because you give so much to others, you sometimes cast your own dreams aside. Yet serving others can often lead to the feeling of fulfillment you seek. The people in your life value, cherish, and support you.

Magical Gifts: Aladar gives you the gifts of altruism, humor, and faith. He is an empathetic guide who will never leave your side in times of trouble.

Keys to Your Success: Realizing that what makes you different is what makes you special.

Aladar's Story: *Dinosaur* (2000)

TWEEDLEDUM AND TWEEDLEDEE

You hold mock battles in your head about what is your best course of action. You aren't weighing the opposing options so much as coming up with ways to make mundane tasks more pleasant. Good-humored and loving, you enjoy the company of those who share your inclinations. You are an idealist and like to surround yourself with beauty and comfort.

Magical Gifts: Tweedledum and Tweedle-dee bestow the gifts of contentment, creativity, and affection. They encourage you to leisurely pursue your idea of the good life.

Keys to Your Success: Having fun daily.

Tweedledum and Tweedledee's Story: *Alice in Wonderland* (1951)

RELAXED
FUN-LOVING
PROTECTIVE

BALOO You have a big heart and a light-hearted attitude. If you could get away with it, you'd fool around all day long. Strong-minded and persistent, you don't let others tell you what to do. You teach what you know best to those who are interested. If the safety of your loved ones is threatened, you become fierce and selflessly defend them.

Magical Gifts: Baloo gives you the gifts of charm, joyfulness, and freedom. He teaches you to have fun, to be serious only when you have to, and to take naps.

Keys to Your Success: Acquiring the bare necessities of life.

Baloo's Story: *The Jungle Book* (1967)

PRINCESS ARIEL You risk everything to pursue your dreams. You long for something far different from what your everyday life has to offer. In your rush to materialize your desires, you ignore the hazards on your path that others cautioned you about. Still, the intensity of your emotions knows no defeat, and you move heaven and earth to be with the one you love.

Magical Gifts: Ariel bestows the gifts of passion, purpose, and transformation. With her help, you will travel to the places where your dreams await you.

Keys to Your Success: Honoring your need to be free while keeping others safe.

Ariel's Story: *The Little Mermaid* (1989)

OCTOBER 9

INCLUSIVE
AWARE
LOVING

CELIA MAE You communicate your thoughts and feelings in a unique and effective manner. You form relationships with others naturally, since you're considerate and make sure that nobody feels left out. You are anything but a pushover: If you feel taken for granted, you might throw a hissy fit. It never lasts long though, and soon you're back to your old charming self.

Magical Gifts: Celia Mae gives the gifts of companionship, confidence, and creativity. Call on her when you need help analyzing a situation from all sides.

Keys to Your Success: Expressing your individuality from your hair to your toes.

Celia Mae's Story: *Monsters, Inc.* (2001)

POSITIVE
SUPPORTIVE
LOYAL

EMILE You enjoy life's simple pleasures. You're a good confidante who in many ways supports those you care about. One of your strengths is recognizing and acknowledging the uncommon abilities of others. As a result, you get to experience new ideas and creations in their beginning stages. Your cheerful disposition and appreciation of life make you a valued friend and family member.

Magical Gifts: Emile brings the gifts of dependability, kindheartedness, and tolerance. When you're trying something new and need encouragement, call on him; he will surely be impressed.

Keys to Your Success: Trusting in ideas you don't readily understand.

Emile's Story: *Ratatouille* (2007)

RELAXED
OBSERVANT
COOPERATIVE

SLEEPY You move at a much slower pace than those around you. In all your activities, you balance work with rest. Your laidback persona doesn't mean you aren't paying attention to the task at hand. Most of the time, you are more perceptive than the average person about what's going on around you. The conclusions you arrive at are sound and border on prophetic.

Magical Gifts: Sleepy bestows the gifts of simplicity, comfort, and a profound dream life. He advises you to follow your body's rhythms and use them to your advantage.

Keys to Your Success: Getting the job done with the right amount of effort.

Sleepy's Story: *Snow White and the Seven Dwarfs* (1937)

MARIE You fantasize about your future. You like attention and want others to notice your special talents. You display your best behavior in public, but when no one is looking you are mischievous and compete for the affection of loved ones. You are highly observant and look for consummate role models to emulate. You're proud and poised, and performing for others makes you happy.

Magical Gifts: Marie bestows the gifts of self-confidence, imagination, and capability. She is certain she can help you show others how wonderful you are.

Keys to Your Success: Knowing how to finish fights resourcefully and innocently.

Marie's Story: *The Aristocats* (1970)

FORCEFUL
TALENTED
DEVOTED

KHAN You are wise, passionate, and strong. You like adventure and challenges that allow you to prove yourself. Admired and valued for your capabilities, you believe it is your duty to support the causes of loved ones. Together, you overcome seemingly insurmountable odds that change the course of history. Love and honor motivate you, and your valiant efforts create new heroes and heroines. You are a noble companion.

Magical Gifts: Khan brings you the gifts of loyalty, courage, and respect. He will provide you with the strength needed to seize your destiny.

Keys to Your Success: Riding on until you and your people are victorious.

Khan's Story: *Mulan* (1998)

WINNIE THE POOH You are sensitive, thoughtful, and instinctual; you do not like to be rushed. You devote your energy toward satisfying cravings. Uncomplicated pleasures appeal to you, and you can be quite clever in attaining them. Generous and gentle, you will always help someone in need. Once you find a place that makes you happy, you're reluctant to leave. You enjoy attending parties with friends.

Magical Gifts: Pooh gives you the gifts of a warm heart, contentment, and purpose. He encourages you to find out what makes you feel wonderful.

Keys to Your Success: Sticking to your plans.

Pooh's Story: *Winnie the Pooh and the Honey Tree* (1966)

OCTOBER 15

CHARITABLE
DYNAMIC
INSPIRED

TONY You are a loving person. You enjoy every moment of your life. Self-assured, you impress others with your big-heartedness and ability to make them feel important. You're a master of your craft and liberally share the results of your work with everyone. You're a sincere, romantic, and entertaining person whose efforts give others poignant and lasting memories of time spent in your company.

Magical Gifts: Tony bestows the gifts of gregariousness, leadership, and imagination. With him as your guide, you will have many reasons to celebrate.

Keys to Your Success: Creating the right ambiance for love.

Tony's Story: *Lady and the Tramp* (1955)

THE UGLY DUCKLING You possess elusive qualities that you don't realize or appreciate right away. Misunderstood by certain people, you can doubt your worthiness. Fortunately, you have a strong spirit and innate knowing that there is a place where you belong and will be happy. When you find that place and enter your new home for the first time, all your sorrow melts way.

Magical Gifts: The Ugly Duckling brings the gifts of self-awareness, pride, and community. He teaches you to honk until your real family hears your call.

Keys to Your Success: Being part of a group in which you feel beautiful.

The Ugly Duckling's Story: *The Ugly Duckling* (1938)

SELF-ASSURED
FIERY
DETERMINED

PRINCESS EILONWY You are confident in your abilities. You possess a healthy dose of self-respect and will stand up for yourself whenever people dismiss your worth. Your curiosity and temper make you fearless in the face of danger. When circumstances warrant, you will work alongside others toward a common goal. You are optimistic, inclusive, and egalitarian and will take the first step to make amends in disagreements.

Magical Gifts: Princess Eilonwy brings the gifts of honesty, sensitivity, and resourcefulness. She encourages you to foster the talents given to you by your ancestors.

Keys to Your Success: Using your training and willpower to achieve your goals.

Princess Eilonwy's Story: *The Black Cauldron* (1985)

BONNIE You love the art of improvisation and the world of make-believe. Original, creative, and intense, you are powerfully good at having fun. Those lucky enough to be part of your private circle adore you. You attract like-minded people who share your interest in uninhibited expression and fun, and they provide you with the knowledge and resources to develop your full potential.

Magical Gifts: Bonnie bestows the gifts of playfulness, kindness, and curiosity. Call on her when you want to reacquaint yourself with the joy and vitality of youth.

Keys to Your Success: Creating a home where everyone feels special.

Bonnie's Story: *Toy Story 3* (2010)

OCTOBER 19

DISTINCTIVE
RESOURCEFUL
DRIVEN

JOHN SILVER You dedicate your life to the pursuit of attaining a cherished dream. Strong and capable, you take the lead in most situations. You have a commanding presence that earns the respect of others. At times you are hard-headed, but once you love someone, they can persuade you to change direction and follow a different path. You are good-natured and humorous.

Magical Gifts: John Silver brings you the gifts of courage, leadership, and charm. He teaches you to be tough when you have to be and soft with those you care about.

Keys to Your Success: Discovering the treasures in your heart.

John Silver's Story: *Treasure Planet* (2002)

DAISY DUCK You are intelligent, intense, and strong-willed. You pay attention to trends and the latest must-haves. It's important for you to make a noticeable impression on others, so you are particular about your appearance and manners. You dislike waiting and angry outbursts, even though you can be just as feisty. You're devoted to friends and loved ones.

Magical Gifts: Daisy gives you the gifts of confidence, passion, and artistic sensibility. She'll help you not only determine what you want but also how to get it.

Keys to Your Success: Knowing that everyone has strengths and weaknesses.

Daisy's Story: *Sleepy Time Donald* (1947)

OCTOBER 21

SENSITIVE
PROGRESSIVE
COLLABORATIVE

BRUCE, CHUM, AND ANCHOR You have a complex nature. You are powerful, perceptive, and intense. It's critical to you that people think well of you, so you try extra-hard to put the wishes of others above your own. Belonging to groups and forming friendships with those who share your altruistic ideals allows you to reveal your true self and deepest desires. All in all, you are a caring soul.

Magical Gifts: Bruce, Chum, and Anchor bring the gifts of loyalty, friendship, and determination. Request their support whenever you seek to develop your highest potential.

Keys to Your Success: Working with others to change problematic behaviors.

Bruce, Chum, and Anchor's Story: *Finding Nemo* (2003)

ESMERALDA People hold a stereotyped image of you based on the role you play in society instead of seeing you for who you really are. Outspoken, you won't tolerate discrimination against others or yourself. You are a compassionate, spirited person who can endure repeated hardships and still keep fighting. Mysterious and defiant, you capture the attention of everyone around you, and they readily listen to your message.

Magical Gifts: Esmeralda bestows the gifts of bravery, empathy, and humor. She will guide you in making ethical decisions and teach you whom you can trust.

Keys to Your Success: Using your magical powers to defeat injustice.

Esmeralda's Story: *The Hunchback of Notre Dame* (1996)

OCTOBER 23

COMMITTED
HEROIC
DEEP

KOVU You are able to rise above any situation and discover what is true for you. Sometimes you find yourself torn between conflicting loyalties and want to run away; but if you stay and face the consequences, your life will improve dramatically. Those who truly love you bring out your ardent and playful nature. Since you make significant sacrifices for loved ones, make sure they have your best intentions in mind.

Magical Gifts: Kovu brings the gifts of transformation, heroism, and devotion. He will guide you through the perils of your past toward a rewarding future.

Keys to Your Success: Determining your own fate.

Kovu's Story: *The Lion King II: Simba's Pride* (1998)

CLEO You enjoy playing a central role in the lives of loved ones. You are observant and communicate your needs through actions more than words. Responsive and caring, you need time to adjust when new members enter your group or family. Once you do, you gain another faithful pal that will adore and nurture you, and vice versa. You are loyal, demonstrative, and aesthetic.

Magical Gifts: Cleo bestows the gifts of affection, luxury, and uncommon companions. She shows you the wisdom in making friends with those in your immediate surroundings.

Keys to Your Success: Loving those different from you.

Cleo's Story: *Pinocchio* (1940)

OCTOBER 25

PARENTAL
COMMANDING
HEART-CENTERED

KING TRITON You are a powerful influence in the lives of others. You have firm beliefs and like to keep chaos at a minimum. Responsible and respectful, you put the needs of others before your own. When you're worried, your temper can get you into trouble, and afterward you regret your actions. Sensitive and affectionate, you can't stay mad for long at those you adore.

Magical Gifts: King Triton gives you commitment, reasoning, and organization. Whenever you feel overwhelmed by obligations, he suggests that you take a respite by the ocean.

Keys to Your Success: Sharing your wisdom with others and then letting them go.

King Triton's Story: *The Little Mermaid* (1989)

COLETTE You are passionate about your profession. A trailblazer, you choose challenging careers that take expertise and grit. Many of your accomplishments become noteworthy. Your intensity can intimidate those who don't know you, but underneath you're sympathetic and supportive of people who respect and value your abilities. You understand the dynamics of a situation and take appropriate action. Perceptive and self-confident, you encourage others to believe in themselves.

Magical Gifts: Colette bestows the gifts of boldness, sensitivity, and inspiration. With her guidance, you can face any barrier and move right through it.

Keys to Your Success: Transforming antiquated systems to manifest your dreams.

Colette's Story: *Ratatouille* (2007)

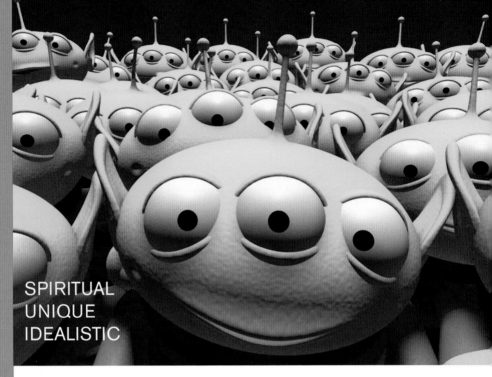

OCTOBER 27

SPIRITUAL
UNIQUE
IDEALISTIC

LITTLE GREEN ALIENS You form strong attachments to people, especially those who have gone out of their way to help you. You imagine a better world and hope to transcend to a higher place where you will know pure joy. Considerate and socially oriented, you are just as elated for the successes of others as you are for your own. New experiences impress and excite you, making every day an intergalactic adventure.

Magical Gifts: Little Green Aliens bring you spontaneity, devotion, and curiosity. Call on them when you need an out-of-this-world escape.

Keys to Your Success: Choosing the destiny that thrills you the most.

Little Green Aliens' Story: *Toy Story* (1995)

EDNA MODE You are creative and desire to use these talents to earn a living. Because you're a visual and practical person, everything you design must meet your demanding requirements. In dealing with others, you are direct and often unaware of the impact of your words. But you're concerned for those you care about and show your love through your actions.

Magical Gifts: Edna bestows the gifts of self-assurance, excellence, and decisiveness. She encourages you to pursue the work you love with passion and purpose.

Keys to Your Success: Using your genius for heroic accomplishments.

Edna's Story: *The Incredibles* (2004)

GIVING
INSPIRATIONAL
HARD-WORKING

JAMES Your actions and ideas profoundly influence the future dreams of your loved ones. Responsible and thoughtful, you take time to nurture those you love. Having goals that you can work toward keeps you motivated, but the life you have now already fulfills you. You lead by example and use your talents to give back to your family and community.

Magical Gifts: James bestows the gifts of creativity, wisdom, and love. Call on him whenever you have forgotten what brings you real joy.

Keys to Your Success: Sharing your vision with others.

James's Story: *The Princess and the Frog* (2009)

TRUSTY You are receptive to the needs of the group; especially your family and those you consider family. Even though you sacrifice your own comfort for loved ones and take pleasure in spending time with cherished friends, you are not a follower. Quite the opposite: You are a leader who leads with your heart. The happiness and well-being of others is what motivates you and drives you to succeed.

Magical Gifts: Trusty brings you the gifts of understanding, good friends, and intuition. He shows you how brave you can be when you channel the energy of love.

Keys to Your Success: Having faith in your instincts.

Trusty's Story: *Lady and the Tramp* (1955)

BRAVE
TALENTED
LOYAL

TIGER LILY You are fearless, powerful, and affectionate. Your feelings run deep, and you would never betray someone you care about. You're feisty and proud, and your actions clearly convey your intentions. You enjoy the forms of creative expression practiced by your ancestors and are artistically adept. Loved and respected by those close to you, you are grateful for the blessings in your life. You are a valued friend and family member.

Magical Gifts: Tiger Lily bestows the gifts of honor, devotion, and originality. Through her teachings, you will discover how to dance your own dance.

Keys to Your Success: Using silence to cleverly defeat your enemies.

Tiger Lily's Story: *Peter Pan* (1953)

SQUEEKS You are capable of profound change. Developing your talents is a solitary pursuit that you vigorously guard. You enjoy taunting those who underestimate your power and wisdom. Though you aren't aggressive, you outsmart your opponents with intelligence and speed, allowing them to succumb to their own foibles. Confident and extraordinary, you manifest your dreams with comfort and elegance.

Magical Gifts: Squeeks gives you the gifts of endurance, humor, and determination. He shows you how to outmaneuver any problem that crosses your path while still having fun.

Keys to Your Success: Staying safe until it's time for you to fly.

Squeeks's Story: *The Fox and the Hound* (1981)

NOVEMBER 2

PRACTICED
TRUSTWORTHY
UNCONVENTIONAL

GEORGE HAUTECOURT You are accomplished and tenured in your chosen career. Because of your extensive experience, people call on you to perform necessary but unusual requests. A bit eccentric yourself, you love to be part of discreet and provocative ventures. Blessed with longevity in everything you do, you have the ability to laugh at yourself and maintain a carefree attitude toward living.

Magical Gifts: George bestows the gifts of a good memory, enthusiasm, and security. He teaches how to be successful in your professional and personal lives.

Keys to Your Success: Staying forever young in mind and in heart.

George's Story: *The Aristocats* (1970)

RESERVED
STRONG
INTELLIGENT

NOVEMBER 3

VIOLET PARR Amazing things happen when you focus your mind on your goal. Too smart and capable to stand on the sidelines and do nothing when someone you care about needs help, you are a brave and fierce defender. Everything you do, you do with intensity; you can run out of energy right in the middle of things. You don't readily admit it, but you are proud of your individuality.

Magical Gifts: Violet gives you the gifts of concentration, wit, and invisibility. Whenever you feel vulnerable, ask Violet to surround you in her force field.

Keys to Your Success: Mastering your innate abilities.

Violet's Story: *The Incredibles* (2004)

MISCHIEVOUS
COMPELLING
HEAD-STRONG

LOCK, SHOCK, AND BARREL You don't mind stirring up a little trouble; in fact, you love it. Intelligent and witty, you are not averse to making promises while crossing your fingers behind your back. You're good at keeping secrets and like to be part of underground missions. Others can count on you to get the job done, but it's better if they don't know the details of how you accomplished it.

Magical Gifts: Lock, Shock, and Barrel give you the gifts of cunning, humor, and dependability. They will help you craft a rebellious strategy to achieve your goals.

Keys to Your Success: Wearing the mask that best reflects who you really are.

Lock, Shock, and Barrel's Story: *Tim Burton's The Nightmare Before Christmas* (1993)

PRINCESS KIDA You are a warrior and defender of life. Interested in endeavors that restore and rebuild fallen structures and societies, you absorb knowledge rapidly, wanting to learn everything you can about the world. You believe that everyone has the right to know the truth, and mysteries intrigue but infuriate you. A wise soul, you are not afraid of change or of sharing your wisdom with others.

Magical Gifts: Princess Kida bestows you with the gifts of longevity, vitality, and enlightenment. She encourages you to unravel the enigmas of the past to create a brighter future.

Keys to Your Success: Reestablishing kingdoms through the blending of information.

Princess Kida's Story: *Atlantis: The Lost Empire* (2001)

DRAMATIC
WISE
EXCITING

MANNY You are energetic and enjoy captivating an audience, large or small. You like to create visual impressions that inspire awe and invoke imagination. Only those special few whom you trust are privy to your methods. Proud and confident, you don't let the fickle opinions of critics dampen your spirit or keep you from achieving. The calm rationality of loved ones allows you to reach your potential.

Magical Gifts: Manny bestows the gifts of aesthetics, dedication, and conviction. Under his guidance, you will truly be able to perform magic.

Keys to Your Success: Entrancing others with a class act.

Manny's Story: *A Bug's Life* (1998)

THE MAGIC CARPET You possess traditional beauty. You are enigmatic and charming, refusing to reveal yourself to just anybody. In fact, you're quite comfortable observing the actions of others without saying a word. Daring and competitive, you're always ready for a challenge. You make friends with those who are just as powerful as you, and together your experiences are unparalleled. In most cases, your actions speak louder than words.

Magical Gifts: The Magic Carpet gives you the gifts of adventure, tenacity, and intelligence. When you are playing games with others, he will teach you the winning strategy.

Keys to Your Success: Taking people on wild rides.

The Magic Carpet's Story: *Aladdin* (1992)

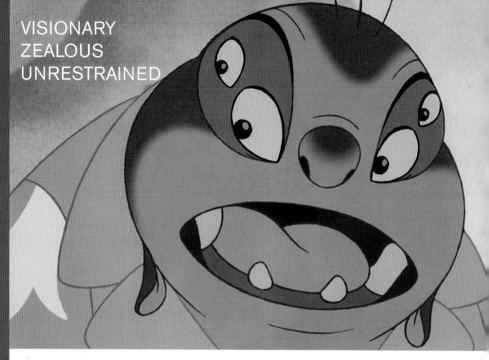

VISIONARY
ZEALOUS
UNRESTRAINED

JUMBA You possess a powerful genius. You loathe limitations, and once you put your mind to something you are unstoppable. This gets you into trouble when you inadvertently disregard the impact of your actions on others. You receive so much joy from your experimentation that you can't imagine living any other way. When people pique your interest, you are eager to assist them. You are strong-willed but compassionate toward others.

Magical Gifts: Jumba gives the gifts of rebelliousness, ingenuity, and expertise. When you want to design something revolutionary, he is there to help you.

Keys to Your Success: Inventing things that have the propensity for good.

Jumba's Story: *Lilo & Stitch* (2002)

PINOCCHIO You are on a journey of discovery, learning about temptation and how to be human. You are committed to understanding what it genuinely means to be good and often learn the answer the hard way. Choosing the easy way out is a disaster for you. After a few troublesome decisions, you realize there is another path to your goals and courageously change course.

Magical Gifts: Pinocchio bestows the gifts of aliveness, wonder, and determination. He wants you to remember that somebody wished for you to be alive.

Keys to Your Success: Telling the truth about what you were doing.

Pinocchio's Story: *Pinocchio* (1940)

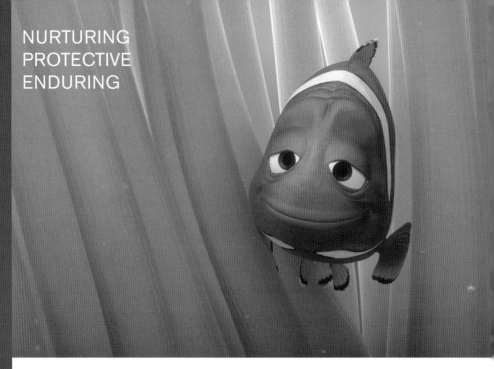

NURTURING
PROTECTIVE
ENDURING

MARLIN You remember the good times and the bad, and those memories influence the choices you make now. You prefer the safety of familiar surroundings, and it's only when a loved one is in danger that you draw on your courage and save the day. Once you have triumphed over your worst fear, real change occurs and life becomes much more fun for you and those you love.

Magical Gifts: Marlin bestows the gifts of commitment, caring, and will-power. Call on him whenever you need encouragement to move beyond the boundaries of your home.

Keys to Your Success: Letting go of the past.

Marlin's Story: *Finding Nemo* (2003)

DENAHI You form deep and lasting bonds with those close to you, and their experiences affect the direction you take in your own life. You enjoy playful joking and retain your sense of humor in even the most arduous circumstances. You're relentless in your pursuit of a goal; it's only when you have exhausted yourself physically, mentally, and emotionally that you ask for help. Needless to say, your love is unconditional.

Magical Gifts: Denahi bestows the gifts of bravery, loyalty, and wisdom. Call on him when you are at a crossroads, unsure of your next step.

Keys to Your Success: Cultivating the wisdom found in all worlds.

Denahi's Story: *Brother Bear* (2003)

GLAMOROUS
LIVELY
KINDHEARTED

FLO You are engaging, cooperative, and sensual. You exhibit traits that people aspire to and find attractive. Looking good is important to you, and you like the attention it brings. You are independent and devote your full energies to whatever profession you're engaged in at the time. Intelligent and outspoken, you are happiest when your work allows you to express yourself and meet new people at the same time.

Magical Gifts: Flo bestows the gifts of practicality, self-employment, and an appreciation for beauty. When you're ready, she'll help you find a place to settle down.

Keys to Your Success: Making sure others don't run out of gas.

Flo's Story: *Cars* (2006)

PEACH You are keenly aware of your environment. Exciting and unusual happenings spark your interest, and you share what you discover with friends. Insightful and focused, you acquire knowledge just by watching people. You're sympathetic to the moods and needs of those close to you and comfort them when they feel lost or scared. Your wit helps you make the best out of any situation and lifts the spirits of those around you.

Magical Gifts: Peach brings the gifts of honesty, individuality, and compassion. Ask for her guidance when your circumstances require perfect timing.

Keys to Your Success: Keeping your mind active.

Peach's Story: *Finding Nemo* (2003)

PERSISTENT
DARING
HELPFUL

ROQUEFORT You possess a heightened sense of awareness. You detect the motivations of others and bravely warn friends and loved ones if you sense any possibility of danger. When things don't go as planned you get flustered, but only temporarily. Soon your courage and resourcefulness kicks in, and you heroically accomplish your intention. You are intense when the situation calls for it, but otherwise caring, polite, and amicable.

Magical Gifts: Roquefort brings you the gifts of loyalty, observation, and refinement. His friendship will provide you with protection and a luxurious home.

Keys to Your Success: Remembering the names of important allies.

Roquefort's Story: *The Aristocats* (1970)

KEKATA You have a deep knowledge of human nature. Without words, you can discern the genuineness of another's character. As a result, your perceptions have a profound effect on people, giving you a prominent place in society. Forceful and honest, you willingly take unpopular stances if doing so will contribute to the greater good of your community. Creative, intense, and skilled, you can unravel mysteries before they occur.

Magical Gifts: Kekata bestows the gifts of prophecy, respect, and healing. He guides you to invoke his help when learning to develop your intuitive medicine.

Keys to Your Success: Seeing and speaking the truth.

Kekata's Story: *Pocahontas* (1995)

OPTIMISTIC
RESOURCEFUL
RESPONSIBLE

KARI You are enthusiastic and self-assured. Although you prepare for jobs by seeking proper training beforehand, on-the-job training brings you unique and intense experiences that test your stamina and reflexes. Each encounter changes you in some way and challenges your thoughts about reality. Even when afraid, you hang in and do your best to keep the situation under control. You are a caring and creative ally.

Magical Gifts: Kari gives you the gifts of dedication, confidence, and bravery. Call on her whenever you find yourself in a tough spot.

Keys to Your Success: Trusting your powerful intuition.

Kari's Story: *The Incredibles* (2004)

LOYAL
WISE
ALTRUISTIC

NOVEMBER 17

TOD You are positively, beyond a doubt, a special person. You are courageous and loving, and no amount of hardship will ever cause you to back down from your word. Having friends you can count on and have fun with is foremost in your life. You transform the hearts of others through your unselfish acts. Forever changed by your example, they become capable of living from a place of compassion instead of hate.

Magical Gifts: Tod gives you the gifts of authentic love, honesty, and kindness. With his guidance, you will discover that real friendship has no enemies.

Keys to Your Success: Knowing what forever means.

Tod's Story: *The Fox and the Hound* (1981)

SUCCESSFUL
SOCIABLE
BRAVE

MICKEY AND MINNIE Your life is full of excitement. Although at times shy, you are happiest when out having fun with loved ones. No matter where you go, you make friends easily and bring laughter to the world. You have many talents, and you try out a variety of vocations, performing each one with proficiency and enthusiasm.

Magical Gifts: Mickey and Minnie bring the gifts of enduring love, universal appeal, and versatility. Call on them when you're looking to start a successful new endeavor and want to have fun doing it.

Keys to Your Success: Working together and having fun.

Mickey and Minnie's Story: *Steamboat Willie* (1928)

POWERFUL
ARTISTIC
DEPENDABLE

THE WARDROBE Experience has taught you a great deal about what is possible if you believe, and your presence alone instills confidence in people. Others benefit from your wisdom and practical abilities, and you offer these graciously. Serious when you have to be, you prefer occupations that allow you the freedom to make up your own rules as you go along. Your sunny disposition influences those around you, leading everyone toward a triumphant outcome.

Magical Gifts: The Wardrobe bestows you with the gifts of strength, inspiration, and maturity. She encourages you to dream big, think big, and act big to fulfill your potential.

Keys to Your Success: Using your creative abilities to guide others.

The Wardrobe's Story: *Beauty and the Beast* (1991)

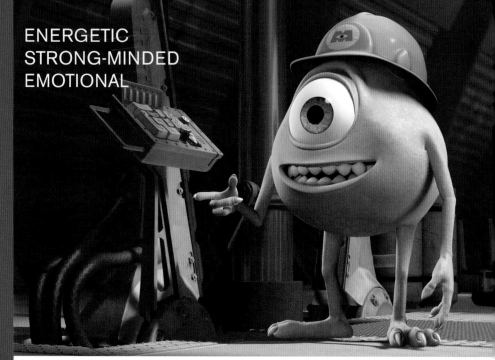

ENERGETIC
STRONG-MINDED
EMOTIONAL

MIKE WAZOWSKI You are full of energy. Although you're loyal and supportive, you aren't afraid to let your friends know exactly how you feel, especially if you believe they are heading in the wrong direction. You are a smooth talker, and you don't mind improvising the truth if it will keep you or someone you care about out of trouble. Expressive and big-hearted, you form lifelong relationships.

Magical Gifts: Mike brings the gifts of intelligence, creativity, and wit. He will stand by you no matter what doors you walk through.

Keys to Your Success: Using your talents to make others giggle.

Mike's Story: *Monsters, Inc.* (2001)

SHANTI You are sensible and convincing. When faced with conflicting information, you tend to believe those who are older and more established. That's because you desire safety, and you focus your attention on keeping everyone, including yourself, free from danger. Your spirited determination enables you to conquer your fears and achieve your objective. You captivate others with your charm and playfulness, and those you attract want to share their world with you.

Magical Gifts: Shanti brings you the gifts of perception, responsibility, and caring. Ask for her guidance when you are exploring wild places.

Keys to Your Success: Discovering your courage.

Shanti's Story: *The Jungle Book 2* (2003)

NOVEMBER 22

CAREFREE
DARING
CHARMING

TRAMP You desire freedom. You don't trust authority since it's let you down in the past. As a result, you make your own rules and live your own life. Fortunately, your wit and finesse get you out of danger. You attract relationships that provide you with stability. Beneath your tough exterior is a protective and demonstrative partner.

Magical Gifts: Tramp gives you the gifts of courage, resiliency, and allure. He shows you how to use these talents to better your life and the lives of those around you.

Keys to Your Success: Letting love, instead of luck, keep you safe.

Tramp's Story: *Lady and the Tramp* (1955)

INTELLIGENT
CREATIVE
STRONG-WILLED

JIM HAWKINS You are smart and intense. Your destiny is to use your talents to become self-aware. Having mentors and loved ones who can help direct your emotional energy into constructive channels helps you reach your potential. Resilient, you learn from your experiences. Your true power comes from your ability to extract the positive from a negative situation.

Magical Gifts: Jim bestows the gifts of ingenuity, forcefulness, and friendship. He reminds you that believing in yourself is the greatest reward.

Keys to Your Success: Knowing the right time to bend the rules.

Jim's Story: *Treasure Planet* (2002)

DETERMINED
FEISTY
PROTECTIVE

PENNY You are able to conquer unpleasant situations through your bravery and imagination. When you need assistance and the usual avenues don't work, you ask for divine guidance and unassumingly send your requests out into the world. People often underestimate your tenacity. You understand animals, and they help you overcome difficulties. Certain objects and possessions make you feel safe, and you guard them at all costs.

Magical Gifts: Penny bestows the gifts of courage, creativity, and spiritedness. She and Teddy will help you realize your dreams and discover what makes you special.

Keys to Your Success: Accepting help in whatever form it comes.

Penny's Story: *The Rescuers* (1977)

Ferrari

TALENTED
LOYAL
CONFIDENT

GUIDO You are persistent, bright, and collaborative. You have extremely particular tastes and choose friends who share them. You never lose sight of your dreams and get excited talking to others about them. Hard working, you practice and perfect your skills. In time, you receive the recognition and the opportunity to show the world that you are the best in your chosen field.

Magical Gifts: Guido bestows you with the gifts of faith, generosity, and expertise. He encourages you to find something that you enjoy doing and to travel to the places that give you the best opportunities for victory.

Keys to Your Success: Possessing abilities understood in any language.

Guido's Story: *Cars* (2006)

INQUISITIVE
ENCOURAGING
OPTIMISTIC

ABBY MALLARD You are gentle, easy-going, and pragmatic. Never losing your poise in uncomfortable situations, you appear unaffected by the insensitivity of certain people. Perceptive, you choose friends who allow you to be yourself. You are wise beyond your years and want to help others solve their problems. When it comes to expressing your own feelings, you can be shy. You have a positive outlook on life and a great sense of humor.

Magical Gifts: Abby bestows the gifts of intelligence, individuality, and empathy. She encourages you to focus on what makes you happy and to go for it.

Keys to Your Success: Encouraging others to seek closure.

Abby's Story: *Chicken Little* (2005)

MUSHU You have lots of energy. You embark on daring adventures to prove your worth to yourself and to others. Your need for approval, respect, and acknowledgment is the initial motivation behind your decisions. Luckily, your compassion for others always wins out over less-than-noble desires. You're confident and rely on intuition in most situations. You're loquacious, and your friends benefit from your humor and companionship.

Magical Gifts: Mushu brings the gifts of courage, spontaneity, and devotion. Call on him when you're in trouble, or when he is the reason you're in trouble.

Keys to Your Success: Being part of the right family.

Mushu's Story: *Mulan* (1998)

UNDERSTANDING MYSTICAL CONSTANT

TANANA You possess spiritual knowledge and bring those teachings into the world. Adept at deciphering signs and symbols, you can communicate complex ideas to others and help those in your community fulfill their destinies. Young people especially ask for your advice because you offer them just enough guidance to help them take the next step. Quirky, direct, and humorous, others respect your position and rely on your love.

Magical Gifts: Tanana bestows the gifts of illumination, awareness, and foresight. She offers you her counsel throughout the cycles of your life.

Keys to Your Success: Knowing that everyone finds their own path.

Tanana's Story: *Brother Bear* (2003)

MEEKO You like to stir things up. You get along best with those who are as free-spirited and daring as you. Your trickster ways can initially upset those who don't know you, but you are bright and know the difference between right and wrong; you just like to test the limits. A faithful and devoted companion, you bring joy and laughter into the lives of loved ones.

Magical Gifts: Meeko brings you the gifts of inquisitiveness, perception, and courage. He will help you get whatever you need if you offer him some biscuits.

Keys to Your Success: Making new friends and teaching them about your home.

Meeko's Story: *Pocahontas* (1995)

CURIOUS
UPBEAT
CLEVER

NIGEL You have an active mind and love the challenge of learning new things. You find the mundane chatter of those around you boring and seek friendships with those you find exciting. Occasionally, you sneak away from your daily routine to mingle with them. Your mischievousness can get you into trouble, but the intention behind your actions is to help those who need you.

Magical Gifts: Nigel bestows the gifts of intelligence, goodwill, and courage. Whenever you need to know important information or the whereabouts of a loved one, he will fly off and find the answer.

Keys to Your Success: Elevating the lives of others.

Nigel's Story: *Finding Nemo* (2003)

ALLURING
BOLD
SELF-ASSURED

BO PEEP You win people over with your magnetic charm. You are strong and influential. Perceptive, you watch what's going on around you and are not afraid to voice your opinion. You worry about the well-being of those you love and can be overly optimistic of their capabilities. When others seek your advice, you are calm and supportive. You are fun to be around and like to rouse the emotions of others.

Magical Gifts: Bo Peep gives you the gifts of observation, kindness, and daring. She encourages you to unabashedly go after what you desire.

Keys to Your Success: Using your crook to get what you want.

Bo Peep's Story: *Toy Story* (1995)

DECEMBER 2

COMPASSIONATE
WISE
POSITIVE

TIMOTHY Q. MOUSE You are a true companion. You bring out the best in people and help them develop talents they didn't know they had. Highly ethical, you question organizations that treat others unfairly. You challenge the insensitive words and actions of others, instilling confidence in those who are bullied. Throughout your life, your personal approach will impact the lives of countless people. Encouraging and kind, you heal people where they hurt the most.

Magical Gifts: Timothy brings the gifts of guidance, shrewdness, and insight. Call on him and he will mentor you toward discovering your distinct potential.

Keys to Your Success: Ensuring happy endings.

Timothy's Story: *Dumbo* (1941)

RAMONE You perfect your creative skills to an unparalleled degree. You are passionate about your vocation and will work at it even if it isn't always lucrative. That's not to say you don't care about compensation for your efforts; but the real reason for your devotion to your craft is because of the gratification it brings. In relationships and in life, you believe in committing yourself to whatever you love the most.

Magical Gifts: Ramone bestows the gifts of craftsmanship, imagination, and concentration. He provides you with the support and desire you need to discover your genius.

Keys to Your Success: Making the world more vibrant.

Ramone's Story: *Cars* (2006)

DECEMBER 4

ORGANIZED
SMART
DISCIPLINED

IRIDESSA You are intelligent and detail oriented. You have good instincts; although you are naturally optimistic, you can sense when a situation will turn out poorly. Persistent, you don't give up until you've mastered the task. Because you worry about outcomes, people who don't take their work as seriously as you can get on your nerves. Not one to hold a grudge, you are always ready to help when needed.

Magical Gifts: Iridessa bestows the gifts of knowledge, vitality, and intuition. Call on her when you're questioning a situation, and she will bring you the right answer.

Keys to Your Success: Creating and capturing rainbows.

Iridessa's Story: *Tinker Bell* (2008)

YEN SID You are confident and know your strengths. Quite often, your talents emerge at a young age; by the time you're grown, they become your vocation. Your wisdom and perceptiveness make you upbeat and quick-thinking in a crisis. When mentoring others, you expect them to follow your directions exactly and don't advance them to the next level until they master the previous one.

Magical Gifts: Yen Sid brings you the gifts of creativity, determination, and focus. He encourages you to work hard to make what you envision a reality.

Keys to Your Success: Sharing your magical abilities with others.

Yen Sid's Story: *Fantasia* (1940)

STRONG-WILLED
ENTERTAINING
HOPEFUL

LADY KLUCK You don't believe in defeat. You have a rowdy sense of humor and poke fun at your rivals. Children and adults are empowered by your encouraging words and bold actions. You believe that love triumphs in all situations. A wonderfully supportive friend, you are someone others definitely want in their court.

Magical Gifts: Lady Kluck gives you the gifts of strength, friendship, and prosperity. Whenever you have doubts about your future success, she will quickly come to your aid and give you many reasons to laugh at your fears.

Keys to Your Success: Knowing how to knock over your opponents.

Lady Kluck's Story: *Robin Hood* (1973)

MORPH You are affectionate, playful, and mischievous. The talents you possess are astonishing and rare. You are visual and receptive to the world around you. Because you mirror and observe what's in your environment, you can adapt to almost any situation. Companionship is vital to your happiness, and you choose friends who are as unique as you. Gentle and empathetic, you nurture those who feel isolated and alone.

Magical Gifts: Morph gives you the gifts of individuality, kindness, and inquisitiveness. He encourages you to use your genius to bring healing to the hearts of others.

Keys to Your Success: Being whoever you want to be.

Morph's Story: *Treasure Planet* (2002)

SOCIAL
FUN
OBSERVANT

SURI You have a big heart. You understand life's hardships and have compassion for those who feel different. Spirited, you aren't afraid to express your views, leaving no doubt in others' minds about how you feel. Being part of a family is important, but you also want to maintain your independence. You are emotional, excitable, and always on the go.

Magical Gifts: Suri gives you the gifts of awareness, sensitivity, and enthusiasm. She encourages you to work with others in establishing a safe place to call home.

Keys to Your Success: Allowing others to take care of you even when you think you don't need it.

Suri's Story: *Dinosaur* (2000)

FROZONE (aka Lucius Best) Your self-assured attitude takes you far. You are daring, witty, and stylish. You play the role of the hero or heroine with ease, although in time you opt for an easy-going existence; you're content to live a less public life, focusing on the needs of those you love. A good friend, sometimes you are too accommodating to the needs of others, allowing their desire for excitement to lure you into trouble.

Magical Gifts: Frozone bestows the gift of supreme coolness, adventure, and imagination. No matter what the season, he'll help you enjoy some winter fun.

Keys to Your Success: Keeping your cool.

Frozone's Story: *The Incredibles* (2004)

SPIRITUAL
COURAGEOUS
INTUITIVE

DECEMBER 10

POCAHONTAS You are open to new ideas and experiences while remaining true to your own values. Strong, noble, and kind, you try to do the right thing, but sometimes your restlessness gets in the way. Interested in the unknown, you delve beneath the appearance of things to understand their true meanings. You possess a genuine love and respect for nature and have a profound connection to everything in life.

Magical Gifts: Pocahontas bestows the gifts of inner strength, wisdom, and determination. With her guidance, you can hear the voice of spirit that dwells inside your heart.

Keys to Your Success: Lovingly helping others overcome their prejudices.

Pocahontas's Story: *Pocahontas* (1995)

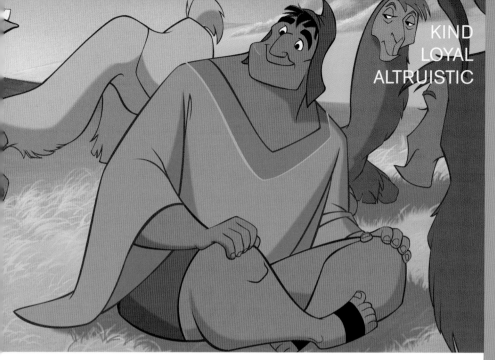

PACHA You believe in the virtue of humanity. You are patient and give people many chances to show their benevolence. Although you don't actively seek adventure, you will rise to the challenge to protect others from harm. You are content with your life and generous with your time and affection. Traditional by nature, you are responsible and perform your duties willingly and cheerfully. Your presence positively influences the behaviors of others.

Magical Gifts: Pacha brings the gifts of humility, gratitude, and integrity. He will guide you toward your potential with understanding and love.

Keys to Your Success: Leading others by example.

Pacha's Story: *The Emperor's New Groove* (2000)

GOOD-NATURED
WITTY
TALENTED

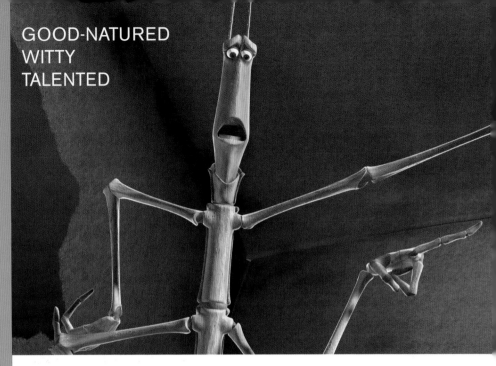

SLIM You are physically expressive and entertaining. Despite successes you have attained, you are always thinking about how you could and should be accomplishing more. It is not enough for you to have the admiration of others; you must find meaning in the duties you perform to feel fulfilled. Committed to your craft, you are excited by opportunities to show others your expertise. You are a loyal and enthusiastic friend.

Magical Gifts: Slim gives the gifts of intelligence, perception, and flexibility. He encourages you to keep expanding your horizons.

Keys to Your Success: Learning to value and enjoy your unintended success.

Slim's Story: *A Bug's Life* (1998)

FRANNY You believe in yourself even when no one else does. Creative and pragmatic, you put in the time and effort to perfect your craft. Unusual people and pastimes appeal to you and make you happy. You are tough and outspoken, refusing to let others push you around. When someone notices you and respects your brilliance, you open your heart to them. People and animals thrive under your care.

Magical Gifts: Franny brings the gifts of acceptance, determination, and individuality. Call on her when you want to master innovative vocations like teaching frogs to sing.

Keys to Your Success: Letting others know what makes you happy.

Franny's Story: *Meet the Robinsons* (2007)

EASY-GOING
SMART
ENTERTAINING

DECEMBER 14

MR. RAY You love to share your ideas and talents with others. Always up for a new adventure, you are curious, observant, and fascinated by how things work. Professionally, you stand out among your peers because of your exuberant and playful style. Children feel comfortable around you, and you are sensitive to their needs, treating them with compassion and respect. You are humorous and knowledgeable and make others feel welcome.

Magical Gifts: Mr. Ray bestows the gifts of exploration, creativity, and optimism. He will take you on a journey to experience and understand the amazing world around you.

Keys to Your Success: Making learning fun.

Mr. Ray's Story: *Finding Nemo* (2003)

ROO You are good-natured, thoughtful, and devoted. There are certain things you want to learn, and you keep trying until you master the skill. You look up to those who are carefree and optimistic, wanting to emulate their behaviors. When you are around people you care about, you like to perform and show off your abilities. Family and friends adore you. You are perceptive and give loving advice.

Magical Gifts: Roo gives you the gifts of wisdom, tenacity, and joy. He encourages you to seek out friends who inspire you.

Keys to Your Success: Having a sense of wonder.

Roo's Story: *Winnie the Pooh and the Honey Tree* (1966)

IMAGINATIVE
DARING
INSTINCTIVE

TARAN You have an active mind and love to daydream. Your thoughts revolve around exciting adventures; as a result, your everyday life seems quite boring. Whenever an opportunity arises for you to prove yourself, you don't hesitate to take it. Intuitive and spontaneous, you are a quick learner committed to realizing your goals. Certain of your abilities, you take on responsibilities that test you to the core.

Magical Gifts: Taran bestows the gifts of willpower, friendship, and vision. Under his guidance, you'll learn what it takes to be a true hero or heroine.

Keys to Your Success: Turning your fantasies into realities.

Taran's Story: *The Black Cauldron* (1985)

FRIEND OWL You pay attention to what's going on in your surroundings. Communicating pertinent information with others and making them feel welcome and special is your intended goal. Your friends appreciate your heartfelt advice even if they don't follow it exactly as you'd planned. Affectionate, friendly, and quirky, you are a valuable member of your community.

Magical Gifts: Friend Owl brings you the gifts of compassion, practicality, and guidance. He encourages you to use your wisdom to make serious situations more enjoyable.

Keys to Your Success: Sharing what you know about twitterpation to those unfamiliar with the concept.

Friend Owl's Story: *Bambi* (1942)

ENCOURAGING
HUMOROUS
PERSISTENT

DAVID You are optimistic and intelligent. Setbacks and roadblocks don't get you down because you're patient and prepared to try again. Never afraid to take opportunities that are beyond what your capabilities at the time, you have a unique sense of humor and an open mind that lets you take life in stride. Having fun and being outdoors enliven you and keep you in shape. You are kind, encouraging, and willing to help people out.

Magical Gifts: David bestows the gifts of wit, compassion, and talent. Ask for his guidance whenever your goals require extra determination and daring.

Keys to Your Success: Knowing that life comes in waves.

David's Story: *Lilo & Stitch* (2002)

THOMAS O'MALLEY You enjoy pushing the limits of what you can get away with. You prize autonomy and put all your energy into maintaining it. Yet there's another side to your devil-may-care attitude, and you gladly commit to a more stable lifestyle when you find someone worthy of the sacrifice. You cherish romance more than adventure and desire love from people you can trust.

Magical Gifts: Thomas gives you the gifts of charm, humor, and altruism. If you're in trouble, he'll show you a million ways to get out of it.

Keys to Your Success: Having the freedom to fall in love.

Thomas's Story: *The Aristocats* (1970)

CURIOUS
KNOWLEDGEABLE
THOUGHTFUL

THE BOY You have a vivid imagination and like to learn. You're interested in people and their behaviors. When presented with conflicting facts, you're quick to discover the truth and reveal it to those involved. You are kind, polite, and bold. In tense situations, you remain calm and can influence the actions of others through your incisive observations. You use your wisdom to help others.

Magical Gifts: The Boy bestows the gifts of study, adventure, and friendship. Ask for his assistance when you want to determine if what you've read is accurate.

Keys to Your Success: Bringing others together in a beneficial way.

The Boy's Story: *The Reluctant Dragon* (1941)

GRANDMOTHER WILLOW You understand the natural order of the world. You listen before speaking and are good at getting others to open up and share what's on their minds and in their hearts. Kind and wise, you help people find their own answers by asking the right questions. When focused, you dislike distractions and make sure everyone respects your need for silence.

Magical Gifts: Grandmother Willow bestows the gift of intuition, mystery, and individuality. She teaches you how to cultivate your inner wisdom to benefit yourself and others.

Keys to Your Success: Teaching others to hear nature's spirit talking.

Grandmother Willow's Story: *Pocahontas* (1995)

HONEST
CONSCIENTIOUS
SELFLESS

BAMBI You have a special role to fill, and you need time to acquire the skills necessary to fulfill your destiny. At a young age, you learned how to take care of yourself, and you admire those who taught you survival skills. You remember every kindness shown to you by others, and they fuel your ambitions. You are intuitive and your dreams provide you with poignant and prophetic information. A powerful defender, you earn the respect of your peers.

Magical Gifts: Bambi bestows you with the gifts of bravery, tenderness, and devotion. He teaches you how to walk alone as well as with others.

Keys to Your Success: Growing into the great person you were meant to be.

Bambi's Story: *Bambi* (1942)

HIRAM FLAVERSHAM You are devoted to your craft and to those you love. You are happiest when you can work autonomously and are free to follow your own ideas. On the outside you appear mild-mannered, but you are willful when provoked. You believe in right and wrong and take your actions and the actions of others seriously. Fond of children, you promote their welfare and merriment.

Magical Gifts: Hiram gives the gifts of ingenuity, compassion, and integrity. He encourages you to retain your childlike wonder and to stand up for what you believe in.

Keys to Your Success: Using your artistic talents to bring joy to others.

Hiram's Story: *The Great Mouse Detective* (1986)

CONCERNED
PROUD
INTENSE

FA ZHOU AND FA LI You try hard to follow the established ways of your family. Admiration and duty are important aspects of your life, and you will do your best to guide your loved ones toward similar success. Even if they choose a different path, you will love them unconditionally. You are loyal not only to your family but to your culture and society as well.

Magical Gifts: Fa Zhou and Fa Li bestow the gifts of respectability, thoughtfulness, and discipline. They will support you in your desire to attain recognition in unconventional ways.

Keys to Your Success: Learning about honor from younger generations.

Fa Zhou and Fa Li's Story: *Mulan* (1998)

TIANA You work tirelessly for what you want and don't wait for things to magically happen. Still, you are a dreamer and listen to the stirrings of your heart. Your life takes you in unexpected directions, but what you obtain in the end is more wonderful than you envisioned. You choose partners with qualities that complement your own; but first they must prove themselves worthy of your affections.

Magical Gifts: Tiana bestows the gifts of independence, intelligence, and warmth. She will guide you toward what you really need to be happy.

Keys to Your Success: Knowing the wishes of your heart.

Tiana's Story: *The Princess and the Frog* (2009)

DECEMBER 26

SERIOUS
CAPABLE
COMPASSIONATE

GRUMPY You like to do things your own way. You have leadership abilities and get cranky when others challenge your authority. You are so determined to be your own person that sometimes people have to coerce you into doing what's best for yourself. Underneath all that complaining is a hero or heroine with a big heart. Try as you might, you can't defend yourself against love.

Magical Gifts: Grumpy doesn't really like to admit he's giving gifts. He says this is the stuff you need to get by: practical skills, hard work, and a courageous heart.

Keys to Your Success: Telling those you love to take care.

Grumpy's Story: *Snow White and the Seven Dwarfs* (1937)

LUMIERE You are clever, talented, and concerned with the happiness of others. Somewhat formal by nature, you want to present a respectable image in social settings. You value your profession and form friendships with those who share your work ethic. Charming, witty, and flirtatious, you lighten the atmosphere in any setting. You generously provide your services to others, and your expertise is beneficial in creating positive changes in your environment.

Magical Gifts: Lumiere bestows the gifts of enthusiasm, assurance, and service. He shows you how to bring light to others without burning yourself out.

Keys to Your Success: Keeping your sense of humor.

Lumiere's Story: *Beauty and the Beast* (1991)

DETERMINED
FEISTY
SELF-ASSURED

JANE You remain poised and confident in challenging situations. You take on tremendous responsibilities that can overwhelm you, but you try not to let it show. You're brave and dependable, qualities that serve you best when you balance them with faith and imagination. Friends and loved ones bring out the best in you by reminding you to have fun. Letting go of preconceived notions fills your life with joy and wonder.

Magical Gifts: Jane bestows the gifts of courage, kindheartedness, and creativity. Call on her when you have forgotten what's possible.

Keys to Your Success: Spending some time in Never Land.

Jane's Story: *Peter Pan in Return to Never Land* (2002)

JIMINY CRICKET You accept prominent roles that profoundly impact the lives of those under your care. A wise and compassionate guide, you do your best to steer others in the right direction. People believe in you, and you are grateful for the opportunities that come your way. Your creativity helps you meet the demands of your job.

Magical Gifts: Jiminy gives you the gift of conscience, common sense, and sincerity. He will make sure you are at the right place at the right time so you can be part of the magic.

Keys to Your Success: Teaching others the difference between right and wrong.

Jiminy's Story: *Pinocchio* (1940)

JIM DEAR AND DARLING You are adept in your profession and provide a nurturing home for your loved ones. You like structure in your personal life, but you have a tender heart; it's easy for those you love to get you to give in to their wishes. Creative, gentle, and affectionate, you are trusting and loyal to family members. After work, you like to relax and have fun.

Magical Gifts: Jim Dear and Darling bestow the gifts of generosity, understanding, and playfulness. They encourage you to enrich your life by sharing it with a beloved pet.

Keys to Your Success: Giving the gift of love.

Jim Dear and Darling's Story: *Lady and the Tramp* (1955)

FLORA You value beauty. You come up with creative solutions to unforeseen problems. Although your ideas are brilliant, you often formulate them without considering the input of your peers. Your intention is to resolve the situation as quickly as possible without ill effects, even if it means keeping certain things hidden. Believing that everything will work out in the end, you ensure that it does.

Magical Gifts: Flora bestows the gifts of ingenuity, diligence, and of course beauty. Whenever you need her help, wear something pink or red and she'll magically appear.

Keys to Your Success: Putting others to sleep until the crisis passes.

Flora's Story: *Sleeping Beauty* (1959)

INDEX OF CHARACTERS

THE LADY AND THE TRAMP
Beaver, September 27
Jim Dear and Darling, December 30
Jock, June 16
Lady, April 23
Tony, October 15
Tramp, November 22
Trusty, October 30

LILO & STITCH
Agent Wendy Pleakley, August 24
Cobra Bubbles, May 5
David, December 18
Grand Councilwoman, May 26
Jumba, November 8
Lilo, February 4
Nani, April 1
Stitch, January 26

THE LION KING
Mufasa, February 22
Nala, May 19
Pumbaa, April 3
Rafiki, June 6
Sarabi, January 25
Simba, August, 18
Timon, September 22
Zazu, August 31

THE LION KING II:
SIMBA'S PRIDE
Kiara, February 12
Kovu, October 23

THE LITTLE MERMAID
Flounder, July 24
Horatio Felonious Ignacious Crus-
    taceous Sebastian, January 31
King Triton, October 25
Prince Eric, July 16
Princess Ariel, October 8
Scuttle, September 5

THE LITTLE MERMAID II:
RETURN TO THE SEA
Melody, January 14

MEET THE ROBINSONS
Franny, December 13
Michael "Goob" Yagoobian, July 21
Lewis, April 13
Wilbur, May 30

MONSTERS, INC.
Boo, February 10
Celia Mae, October 9
Mike Wazowski, November 20
Roz, September 26
Sulley, September 29

MULAN
Cri-Kee, July 13
The Emperor, April 22
Fa Zhou and Fa Li, December 24
Grandmother Fa, March 29
Khan, October 13
Li Shang, January 11
Mulan, July 27
Mushu, November 27

OLIVER & COMPANY
Dodger, August 1
Georgette, May 17
Jenny, April 27
Oliver, June 27
Rita, July 17

PETER PAN
George and Mary Darling, May 18
The Lost Boys, March 7
John Darling, September 16
Michael Darling, June 29
Nana, March 11
Peter Pan, June 13
Tiger Lily, October 31
Tinker Bell, June 21
Wendy, July 7

PETER PAN:
RETURN TO NEVER LAND
Danny, March 2
Jane, December 28

PINOCCHIO
The Blue Fairy, March 16
Cleo, October 24
Figaro, January 29
Geppetto, July 9
Jiminy Cricket, December 29
Pinocchio, November 9

POCAHONTAS
Chief Powhatan, June 17
Flit, May 29
Grandmother Willow, December 21
John Smith, April 17
Kekata, November 15
Meeko, November 29
Nakoma, August 12
Pocahontas, December 10

THE PRINCESS
AND THE FROG
Charlotte La Bouff, July 11
Eli "Big Daddy" La Bouff, August 30
Eudora, June 30
James, October 29
Louis, May 22
Mama Odie, January 23
Prince Naveen, June 15
Princess Tiana, December 25
Ray, September 24

RATATOUILLE
Auguste Gusteau, April 15
Colette, October 26
Django, July 8
Emile, October 10
Linguini, September 9
Remy, February 11

THE RELUCTANT DRAGON
The Boy, December 20
The Dragon, July 2
Sir Giles, January 15

THE RESCUERS
Bernard, September 4
Bianca, October 3
Evinrude, March 31
Orville, May 28
Penny, November 24
Rufus, February 18

THE RESCUERS DOWN UNDER
Cody, February 25
Jake, January 21
Marahute, June 12

ROBIN HOOD
Allan-a-Dale, May 24
Lady Kluck, December 6
Little John, May 9
Maid Marian, May 1
Robin Hood, August 8
Skippy, August 13

SLEEPING BEAUTY
Fauna, May 23
Flora, December 31
Merryweather, February 1
Prince Phillip, May 21
Princess Aurora, March 20

SNOW WHITE
AND THE SEVEN DWARFS
Bashful, June 22
Doc, June 18
Dopey, March 24
Grumpy, December 26
Happy, April 16
The Prince, August 10
Sleepy, October 11
Sneezy, January 5
Snow White, March 6

SWORD IN THE STONE
Archimedes, May 31
Merlin, June 5
Sir Ector, September 7
Wart (young King Arthur), March 4

TIM BURTON'S
THE NIGHTMARE
BEFORE CHRISTMAS
Jack Skellington, May 11
Lock, Shock, and Barrel, November 4
Sally, February 8

TINKER BELL
Blaze, March 17
Clank and Bobble, January 27
Fairy Mary, April 19
Fawn, May 14
Iridessa, December 4
Queen Clarion, September 25
Rosetta, August 25
Silvermist, March 3
Terrance, June 4

TOY STORY
Andy, July 5
Bo Peep, December 1
Buzz Lightyear, January 24
Hamm, October 2
Little Green Aliens, October 27
RC, August 2
Rex, August 14
Wheezy, September 13
Woody, February 6

TOY STORY 2
Jessie, June 10

TOY STORY 3
Bonnie, October 18

TREASURE PLANET
B.E.N., June 20
Captain Amelia, August 5

Doctor Doppler, August 26
Jim Hawkins, November 23
John Silver, October 19
Morph, December 7

UP
Carl, January 4
Dug, June 23
Ellie, August 22
Kevin, August 19
Russell, May 20

WALL•E
The Captain, February 2
Eve, August 16
Wall•E, September 10

THE WILD
Bridget, July 31
Ryan, March 14
Samson, January 12

WINNIE THE POOH
AND THE HONEY TREE
Christopher Robin, August 21
Eeyore, January 2
Gopher, January 22
Kanga, June 25
Owl, July 14
Rabbit, September 14
Roo, December 15
Winnie the Pooh, October 14

WINNIE THE POOH AND THE
BLUSTERY DAY
Piglet, July 10
Tigger, March 25

WYNKEN, BLYNKEN, & NOD
Wynken, Blynken, & Nod, March 12

ACKNOWLEDGMENTS

To all those who believe . . .
Especially,
Brian, my beloved prince, for giving me true love's kiss.
My fairy godmothers, Laurie and Cindy, for helping me keep the magic alive.
And to Jason, the sorcerer, for giving me the power of opportunity.

ADDITIONAL COPYRIGHT NOTICES